MINE

Also by Courtney Cole and Gallery Books

Saving Beck

MINE

courtney cole

G

Gallery Books

New York London Toronto Sydney New Delhi

G

Gallery Books
An Imprint of Simon & Schuster, Inc.
1230 Avenue of the Americas
New York, NY 10020

First Gallery Books trade paperback edition May 2019

GALLERY BOOKS and colophon are registered trademarks of
Simon & Schuster, Inc.

For information about special discounts for bulk purchases, please contact Simon & Schuster Special Sales at 1-866-506-1949 or business@simonandschuster.com.

The Simon & Schuster Speakers Bureau can bring authors to your live event. For more information or to book an event, contact the Simon & Schuster Speakers Bureau at 1-866-248-3049 or visit our website at www.simonspeakers.com.

Interior design by Alison Cnockaert

Manufactured in the United States of America

10 9 8 7 6 5 4 3 2 1

Library of Congress Cataloging-in-Publication Data

Names: Cole, Courtney (Novelist) author.
Title: Mine / Courtney Cole.
Description: First Gallery Books trade paperback edition. | New York : Gallery
    Books, 2019.
Identifiers: LCCN 2018051354 | ISBN 9781501184543 (trade paper) | ISBN
    9781501184550 (ebook)
Subjects: LCSH: Domestic fiction. | BISAC: FICTION / Contemporary Women. |
    FICTION / Literary.
Classification: LCC PS3603.O42825 M56 2019 | DDC 813/.6—dc23
LC record available at https://lccn.loc.gov/2018051354

ISBN 978-1-5011-8454-3
ISBN 978-1-5011-8455-0 (ebook)

To all the women who have had their hearts shattered.
Trust me, you will be stronger in the end.

MINE

one

TESSA

My phone dings with that high-pitched *tinggg* of an in-coming text message. I ignore it, focusing on the road instead.

My Jaguar smells like feet, carnival food, and . . . what is that? *Gouda? Ball sweat?* I glance into the rearview mirror and meet the hazel gaze of my middle child, Connor, his tawny-brown hair mussed from sleeping. At eighteen, with his teenage hormones, lack of concern for cleanliness, and endless appetite, he's the most likely culprit.

"Con, why does it smell like hot dogs in here?" My fingers are numb on the wheel, a product of driving two hundred and fifty miles to Atlanta, and I flex them tiredly. Thank Jesus, we're almost there.

Connor yawns and shoves his sleeping sister off him. Ava slumps against the door instead, without even waking up, another gift of being a teenager. At fifteen, she sleeps without a care in the world.

The back seat is loaded down with pillows, blankets, and everything the two of them could possibly need for three weeks at their grandparents', a yearly trip that, thankfully, they haven't outgrown. It would crush my parents otherwise.

Connor holds up a sack of corn chips. "Maybe it's this." He lifts his long, tanned leg high in the air and wiggles his bare toes. "Or this." He cackles.

I sigh. "Did you get crumbs everywhere?"

"Probably," he answers cheerfully. "Are we almost there?"

"Yep. About ten minutes. Can you wake your sister?"

I regret the words as soon as they're out of my mouth. Connor grabs a pillow and tackles Ava with it, covering her head and jabbing his strong fingers into her rib cage until she shrieks.

"Mom!" she screams, gasping for air. "Make him stop. God, *get off*, Connor."

"Kids, we're almost there. Give me a break, please."

They roughhouse for a minute or two more and then sit back on their respective sides of the car.

"Thank you," I tell them. Ava is grumbling, trying to fix her long hair, the exact same shade as Connor's, which is the exact shade of my husband's.

"You're a beast," she announces to her brother. He laughs, unconcerned.

I nose the car down the road, a shadowy lane covered by a canopy of oak trees draped in Spanish moss, that leads to my childhood home. It is the quintessential depiction of picturesque southern living.

Three more minutes.

My phone buzzes again in my purse against the floorboard.

2

I fight the urge to grab it. My type-A personality makes it hard not to deal with things immediately as they come in, but I made a promise to the kids years ago that I wouldn't look at my phone in the car, not even at red lights. I have to set a good example. No texting and driving. It's hard, though. Between my business and my kids and my husband and my mom . . . my phone has become an appendage.

"Oh my God. Connor!" Ava covers her nose with a blanket and buries her head beneath it, and before I can even ask, I smell the answer.

"Connor," I groan. "We're almost there. Hold it in!"

Connor shrugs. "You shouldn't have stopped for burritos for lunch," he tells me. "Oh, hey! There's Pops!"

I turn my attention from the rancid odor to my dad, who is bending over a rosebush in the front yard. He straightens as we pull into the drive, and his wrinkled face stretches into a grin. Warmth floods my belly at the sight of him, familiar and tall.

Ava leaps out of the car and bounds into his arms. Connor isn't far behind. If nothing else, my kids are affectionate. I park the car and get out, stretching my legs and rubbing my back. I'm definitely not twenty anymore. My body feels every mile of this road trip.

"Peanut!" Dad calls to me. I love that he stills uses my childhood name. I'm forty years old, but to my father, I'll forever be a little girl with pigtails and a red Kool-Aid mustache.

"Daddy." I breathe in deeply as he hugs me tight. He smells like peppermint, as always. I hear my mom on the front porch, and soon, we're all tumbling inside, chattering as we drag in the kids' luggage.

"I'm so disappointed Colt couldn't come this year," my mom clucks, her finely arched eyebrows knit together. "He's in college, not on the moon. Colleges let out for the summer."

"Mom, he has an internship," I remind her. "It's a huge opportunity. He couldn't pass it up."

"But what about his meds?" she asks, and her voice is a bit thin. She's worried, like I was when Colt first pitched the idea to Ethan and me. "What if he forgets?"

"Mom, he won't. He's been taking them his entire life. And he knows what happens if he doesn't."

He knows he could die.

"Nonnie, he misses you," my daughter assures her. "He hates that this is the first summer he won't be here. He wants us to FaceTime him tonight."

That appeases my mom, but she sniffs. "You'll have to help," she tells Ava. "I don't know how to do that." She bustles into the kitchen, and my dad looks at me.

"You're not staying overnight, are you?" he asks, noticing that amid the mountain of luggage, there isn't a suitcase for me.

"I can't, Dad. Ethan will be home tonight. He's been in New York for a couple of weeks, and we're going to spend the weekend together. It's been a long time. We need it, trust me."

Dad nods, understanding like always. "Ethan does work hard," he agrees. "And so do you. Don't forget to slow down sometimes."

"I won't, Dad."

My phone rings in my pocket, and my dad stares pointedly at me. I grimace and look at the screen. It's my assistant. I let it go to voicemail.

"Daddy, I love you," I say and kiss his cheek. He grins.

"Nice try, but that's not gonna work," he answers. "I'm not gonna be the one to tell your mom."

I groan as my father pulls me into the kitchen. He opens their fridge, pours me freshly squeezed lemonade, and pushes it into my hands. Then he sits on a stool at the breakfast bar and waits . . . for the show, I assume.

I sigh.

My mother is putting together thick ham and cheese sandwiches for the kids, because she always thinks I don't feed them enough. Neither of my ingrates have bothered to tell her that they've eaten twice already on the five-hour trip from Florida. Ava winks at me behind my mom's back, and I roll my eyes.

Good lord.

"Do you want one, Tessa?" my mother asks, piling a thick layer of tomatoes and lettuce on the sandwiches. Ava, who would complain incessantly about those vegetables at home, keeps silent, angelic.

"No, thanks, Mom," I answer. "I . . . um . . ."

"Mom has to go straight home," Ava interrupts. "She's going to meet Dad."

My mom stops what she's doing.

"What do you mean, you have to meet Ethan? Where is he?"

Her brown eyes bore into my own, and I swallow hard. Why is it that even at forty, my mom's judgment still makes me squirm?

"He's been in New York working on a project," I answer calmly. "You know he has to travel."

She goes back to the sandwiches, obvious disapproval plastered on her face. Through pinched lips, she mutters, "You need to watch that."

"Watch what, Mom?" I ask, unable to keep the humor out of my voice. She pauses and lifts an eyebrow sharply.

"You need to take care of your husband, Tessa. You get too distracted with your job. You have to take care of him, too!"

My head almost snaps back.

"How is his business trip somehow a reflection on me?" I ask incredulously. "He's the one with the projects in New York, Mom."

"And you're the one who was out in LA a few weeks ago," she counters, slapping the tops on the sandwiches and handing one to each kid. My dad holds out a hand, and she ignores him. "You're the one who was in Hong Kong the month before that."

"Only for a week," I say slowly. "Ethan was home with the kids. I have a company to run, too, Mom, and I've worked hard to get it where it is today. Are you saying that since Ethan has to travel so much, I should stay at home and give up my dreams?"

Mom sighs and washes the knife in the sink.

"Why do you have to make everything so dramatic?" she asks with a sigh. "I'm not saying you should give anything up. But when you started your business . . . it was supposed to be *little*. A small home-based thing where you could make some money when the kids were young. It wasn't meant to become this huge company that takes you away from your family all the time."

I'm sputtering, trying to think of a counter argument for my mother's old-fashioned ideas, when Connor speaks up, his mouth full of ham.

"Nonnie, honestly, we don't mind. When she's gone, we get to order out. It's a win–win."

My mother turns to stare at me.

"See? Your kids have to order out when you're gone. They're going to grow up with brittle bones."

I look at Connor and Ava, at their long limbs and strong, lean bodies, both the product of school athletics and surfing, and level a gaze at my mother.

"They're hardly malnourished, Mom." I clear my throat and weigh my words before I continue. "First, you're right. I started out making organic makeup in my house because I wanted a side business to feel like I was contributing to the family. I know you know what it's like to not help financially, and I didn't want that stress."

My mom has the grace to flush. She was a stay-at-home mom for years, and while she loved being with my brother and me, she has mentioned that she would've liked to have taken a bit of the burden off my father.

"Second," I continue. "There was—and is—a need. Women really do care what they put into their bodies. They want choices. They want to know that the stuff they're putting on their skin isn't full of chemicals or being cruelly tested on animals."

"So you're saying you built this huge company for altruistic reasons?" my mom asks, still flushed. I cringe a little because I probably shouldn't have called her out like that. I know she's sensitive about it.

"No, of course not," I admit. "I do want to make a difference, and I do want women to have a healthy choice. But I also want to make money. I want to be successful. That's not a crime, Mom."

"Blush made eighty-seven million last year," Ava breaks in. She's proud of me, and that calms my ruffled feathers. I'm driven by a need to be a positive example for my daughter, and I want her to know she can do anything she sets her mind to.

"That's gross sales, honey," I remind her. "That's before all of the expenses and stuff are taken out."

"Still," she says firmly. "Mom's a rock star. She got interviewed in *Marie Claire* last month."

I blush and shake my head. "Okay, enough shop talk!" I tell them. "Suffice it to say, Mom, that I have a good job. I've worked for it, and my kids are not neglected."

My mother sniffs again. "Well, I should hope not. That's not the way you were raised."

My father glances over his shoulder, away from where he is making his own sandwich. "Peanut, looks like there are storm clouds rolling in. If you're going to head home tonight, you might want to go now."

I look out the window, and sure enough, the sky is darkening.

"Okay. Come here, kids." I open my arms, and they both fold in. Ava is almost as tall as me, but Connor, at six feet, four inches, towers over us. He doesn't hesitate to wrap his arms around both of us, and I feel the tension draining away as I release the power of my mom's words. I'm raising my kids differently than she raised me, but they're turning out pretty amazing. I feel their hearts beating next to mine at this very second.

I kiss them both.

"I love you guys," I tell them as I breathe in the scent of my daughter's strawberry shampoo. "More than life. Connor, don't antagonize your sister. Ava, get out of bed before noon. Promise?"

They sort of nod and sort of ignore me before going back to their sandwiches and chattering with my dad.

I turn to my mom. "Mom, thank you for having the kids. I hope you have a great time."

She nods, and despite her standoffishness, I still hug her.

"I love you guys," I call as I turn to leave. My mom doesn't say it back, because she's uncomfortable with emotion, but my dad and the kids do. I don't hold it against her. She comes from a long line of distant women who don't wear their feelings on their sleeves. *Never let them see you sweat, dear, or they'll think they have the power.* I've heard that for as long as I can remember. And honestly, it does come in handy sometimes, in business.

When I'm back in the car, I check my phone. Two missed calls from Ethan and more than a few missed calls from my assistant, Carrie, followed up by texts.

Have you decided on the new colors for the fall lipstick palette? We need to get them to the printer for the catalogue.

Tessa! Are you ignoring me?

I answer quickly, eyeing the approaching storm. Thunder booms as I type a response. *Yes, I've decided. I'll email you tonight when I get home.*

I dial Ethan's number. It rings and rings and goes to voice-mail.

He must already be on the plane.

"Hey, babe. I'm just leaving my folks' house. I'll be home in a few hours. Love you!"

I drop my phone back into my purse and roll the windows down for the first mile or two to air the car out. The scent of the storm chasing me fills the car with earthy cleanliness, eliminating all traces of Connor's lunch.

I lean my head back and drive in silence, the first I've had in weeks and a luxury I don't usually enjoy. For once, I don't feel guilty for buying such an expensive car for myself. The butter-soft leather seat enveloping me into its softness really does take the sting out of a long trip. It's not like we can't afford it. I was just raised to not be extravagant, and sometimes, our lifestyle makes me feel guilty when it shouldn't. We've worked hard for what we have.

I drive in silence until I've only got forty-five minutes to go and can't stand it any longer. Reaching down, I turn on the radio.

It doesn't take long to hear the news.

"Tropical Storm Fiona has taken a turn and is projected to be a category two hurricane by midnight. It will hit landfall by morning and will likely become a category three by then."

Damn it. I thought it was just a normal summer storm. I'd been so distracted getting the kids ready to go, I hadn't even been paying attention. I groan aloud and break my own rule about using the phone in the car. I jab a button on the steering wheel and use voice command.

"Call Ethan," I instruct. The phone rings over Bluetooth, and I expect to get my husband's voicemail. But I don't. He answers on the fifth ring, out of breath.

"Hey, honey," he greets me.

"Hey," I answer, startled. "I thought you were on the plane."

"Then why are you calling me?" he teases. I roll my eyes.

"I was just going to leave you a message. That tropical storm is turning into a hurricane. I'm about forty-five minutes from home. Did your flight get delayed?"

"Errr, no," Ethan answers, hesitant now. I recognize the tone when he doesn't want to tell me something, and I tense up immediately.

"What?" I demand.

"I have to stay another day."

"What? Why? Ethan . . . we were supposed to spend the weekend together. We haven't been able to for a hundred years, and now there's a storm . . . and I'll have to take care of everything myself!"

I'm annoyed, and before I even hear his reply, I know what he's going to say.

He has to work. Again.

And while I should understand, because I'm busy, too, it seems that he's been busier and busier lately. And I've been left more and more often to do everything on the home front.

"Babe, I was able to get a meeting to bid for that project in Charleston. The investor is here in the city for tonight only. It's a thirty-million-dollar job."

He's earnest and he's right. But I'm annoyed anyway.

I think of the work to be done at home, the emails I need to answer, the calls I need to make because of the fall catalogue, and none of it can wait. It wears me out just thinking about it, especially since I've been on the road all day and my forty-year-old bones are stiff.

"I'd been planning to finish work up tonight and then take

the rest of the weekend off with you," I tell him, unable to keep the disappointment out of my voice. "I got special underwear and everything."

"Now you have my attention."

"I should hope so. But now I have to stormproof the house."

"Babe, I'm really sorry," Ethan says, and I can tell he's sincere. "I swear, I'll make it up to you. A back rub, foot rub, breakfast in bed, whatever you want. I'll even model your new underwear for you if you want."

The thought of my manly husband prancing around in lacy black underthings makes me burst out laughing. He laughs, too, and he knows he's forgiven.

"Fine, whatever," I finally say, trying to be annoyed again. "But you know that if it really does turn into a hurricane, flights will be canceled tomorrow. You'll miss the whole weekend."

"I'm sorry," he tells me softly. "I really am. I love you. I'll get home as soon as I can. I promise."

"Okay," I relent. As I always do. I love him, his mossy hazel eyes, tanned skin, long legs, and cocky grin. I've loved him since the moment I laid eyes on him my freshman year in college. "You owe me, though," I grumble.

He laughs. "I always owe you." I have to agree on that one. "Hey, drive safely," he says, serious now. "Is it raining yet?"

As if on cue, fat raindrops start hitting the windshield.

"Yep," I answer.

"Okay. Pay attention to the road. I'll call Colt and make sure he's good for the weekend, that he's got enough meds and food and whatnot. You know he's safe in the FSU dorms, so don't worry about that. The worst that can happen is their power will go out."

"I know," I tell him. "He'll be fine. Just remind him to make sure he has enough meds to last the entire weekend just in case."

"I will. Don't worry. Call me when you get home."

"I will. Love you."

"Love you, too."

I press End, and the rain gets worse. The thing about Florida is that a storm can go from *nothing* to *something* to *all hell is breaking loose* in no time at all. The radio plays on, warning about the dangers of the coming storm.

"Winds from Fiona are currently clocking in at seventy-five miles per hour," the weatherman announces. *"This storm has the potential to be very dangerous. Watch the storm cone, and if you are in the affected area, take immediate precautions."*

By the time I take the exit for Santa Rosa Beach, I'm already in storm mode and thinking about the provisions I have at home. I know we've got cases of water in the garage, extra batteries on hand for the flashlights, and canned soup in the pantry, so I don't need to stop at the store. I head for home, listening to the rushing water hit the bottom of my car doors.

Freaking Mother Nature.

When I turn down the long, lonely road that leads to our house, I see a pair of headlights emerge from the opposite direction, and I recognize my neighbor Millie's car. I edge to a stop and roll my window down as the rain pelts in.

"Are you leaving?" I yell above the din, the rain soaking my hair and the inside of my car.

She nods, trying to shield her face. "Ed's already up north, so I'm going to head up there for the week. Susan and Bob left this morning. You're not leaving? They say this might be a big one, maybe even a cat four or five. Where's Ethan?"

"New York."

"You should go, Tess," she urges. "You'll be alone here. Everyone on the street is gone."

The rain pelts harder now, and it makes no sense to keep trying to talk.

"Be safe, Millie!"

She waves at me, and I roll my window up. Son of a bitch.

My tires slide a little, hydroplaning before the rubber finally catches, and I turn onto my brick driveway. My home rises out of the ground in a giant mass of stucco and windows, and the realization that I'll be weathering a hurricane alone suddenly hits me.

For a brief minute, I ponder turning around and heading inland somewhere, anywhere, but the rain has gotten so heavy that I can't even see Millie's taillights. And the storm isn't even inland yet. It really wouldn't be safe. Plus, I've weathered a dozen storms over the past few years. It doesn't matter that I'm alone.

I open the garage door and pull inside, and instantly, the noise stops. I exhale, then shiver as goosebumps form on both of my arms, from elbow to shoulder.

I wipe down the inside of my car door, running a towel over the Italian leather, and then stare out through the open garage door.

Everything is whitish gray, and the rain hits the ground so hard it bounces and looks like hail.

I sigh as the thunder booms, shaking the ground beneath my feet, and I take one brief moment to feel sorry for myself before I get to work.

As an architect, Ethan designed us a beautiful house that graces the bluffs overlooking the ocean.

But it has forty-five windows.

Forty-five.

Which means I'll have to climb the giant extension ladder forty-five times in the pouring rain. I'm cursing Ethan's name already.

The ladder is heavy, but I manage to pull it down from the hooks in the garage and drag it around the side of the house, something that is usually a two-person job. My hands are slippery as I climb the metal rungs, but I get to the top, pull the shutters closed on Ava's bedroom window, and slide the reinforcement bar across them. I step down, and slip. Startled, I grab at the ladder and hang on for dear life. It's wobbly because I didn't wedge it very well at the bottom. Because, usually, there's someone down there holding it.

Son of a bitch.

I steady myself, climb down amid the wind that threatens to blow me off, and start again. I'm on autopilot, and it takes me an hour.

On my last window, there is a crack of lightning so close that I feel my life flash before my eyes, and I scramble down from the metal ladder as fast as I can. I want to leave it here, instead of lugging it back inside the garage, but with gale-force winds, it could become a projectile and blow through my shutters. So, summoning the last bit of my strength, I drag it to the garage and collapse on the steps that lead into the house.

My legs are rubbery, my arms are shaking, and dear God, I'm tired. When I open my eyes, the two shiny gas cans catch my eye. A bad feeling sinks in as I stand up, walk over, and shake one, finding it empty. Hesitantly, I lift the other.

Also empty.

Goddamnit. The generator won't have gas. Ethan left the cans empty. During hurricane season. *What was he thinking?*

I pull my phone out of my wet pocket, and dial his number with fingers so tired, they shake. I get his voicemail.

"I'm home. I got all the shutters closed, but you left the gas cans empty." I can't keep the accusation out of my voice. If I lose power—and I will—I'll be the one here in the dark alone. He'll be living it up in New York in a posh hotel room with A/C. "Anyway, I'm home. Call me when you can."

I hang up and head for a hot shower. Without a generator, it might be the last one I get with the lights on for a day or two. There's nothing worse than showering in the pitch black.

I head for our room at the end of the hall, just past the living room. The master bedroom took Ethan the longest to design. It faces the ocean, with magnificent views of the water. Normally. Right now, the shutters are closed, boxing me in. I flip on the light, and a soft romantic glow emits from the tray ceiling, a feature Ethan is proud of.

I strip off my soaked clothing and drop them in a heap on the stone tiles of the walk-in shower.

Standing with my hands against the stone, I allow the hot water from all four showerheads to beat down on my shoulders and back, warming me up. I usually only use one because it makes me feel guilty to use all of that water. But with the rain pelting down outside like it is, I doubt it's a problem.

Twenty minutes later, I pull on yoga pants and a soft shirt and towel-dry my blond hair.

Padding down the hall, the house seems like a massive mausoleum, devoid of outside light. I feel so secluded, like I'm in a bubble, and when I lose power, it will feel even more so. My hands are still shaky from climbing the ladder when I pour a glass of wine and gather some candles and the long-handled lighter.

I'm listening to the ocean slam into the beach and the wind howl against the house, when my phone rings.

"Mom, are you okay?" Ava asks worriedly. "We've been watching the weather. It's gonna get bad."

"I know, honey. But I've gotten the house all closed up, and I'm fine," I assure her. "Don't worry."

"What about Colt, though?"

"He'll be safe and sound in his dorm room. *Don't worry.*"

As we talk, I walk around, hunting for my iPad so I can answer emails and charge my phone when Ava and I hang up. But I don't see it anywhere.

"Sweetheart, have you seen my iPad?"

She's silent for a beat. "Um, I have it."

"You packed mine? Why not your own?"

"Because I couldn't find mine."

"Again? *Ava*, you have to take better care of your stuff."

"I know, I'm sorry, Mama." She always breaks out the "mama" when she's in trouble or wants something, and honestly, it usually works. "I should let you go so you can finish prepping. Stay safe, okay?"

"I love you, Ava. Don't worry. Everything is fine. But when you get home, you're finding that iPad."

I hang up, plug my phone into an outlet in the kitchen, and head to Ethan's study to get his iPad. I find it balanced on a stack of file folders on his desk, and I grab it, heading back out to the living room.

I switch on the lamps, curl up on the sofa, and pull a blanket over my lap as his iPad dings with an incoming text message, that oh-so-familiar *tinggg*.

In a trained response to that sound, I look at the message.

And then I freeze.

I want to fuck you. When can I see you again?

The next moment is simultaneously confusing and crystal clear. My mind is bending and freezing everything in place as I struggle to comprehend what I'm looking at, *because the text isn't for me*.

I scroll through the thread and find several pictures of a young, fit, and *naked* woman. And the texts . . . from her to him, from him to her . . . streaming in from Ethan's iPhone, which is paired with this iPad.

The room spins as reality sinks in.

This can't be real. But I'm staring at the words, at the proof, and my stomach heaves.

My husband is having an affair.

two

LINDSEY

I look at the lingerie I've laid out on the bed. Red, scalloped, and lacy, it will accent my hips and flat stomach. I've lathered on vanilla lotion—they say vanilla is an aphrodisiac for men, and if that's true, he won't be able to keep his hands off me.

Given our texts over the past couple of weeks, I doubt we'll need much help in that department, but this is the first time I'll be meeting Nicholas in person. I don't want to take any chances.

I grab my purse and head out the door, pausing only to google the address of the bar where Nicholas wants to meet.

My phone is on my lap when his text comes in. I look at it and smile.

Is it dumb that I'm nervous?

Hell, no. I'm nervous, too. What if he's not who he's pretending to be? What if I've been catfished? I don't say these things, though. Because I want the appearance of total confidence.

I prop my phone on my steering wheel so I can answer and still see the road.

It's flattering, I reply. *I'll be there in ten. I promise I won't bite. Probably.* ☺

My heart lifts as I continue driving. He's definitely into me. My radar wasn't off. I look down at my phone again and see my destination is 0.2 miles away on my right.

I look around, confused. There's nothing here but a dilapidated old building in a dusty parking lot. He said it was a hole in the wall, but to say it's out of the way is an understatement. It's small, dingy, and two of the lights in the Miller Lite sign in the window are out. "Miler Lie." A runner with secrets.

I park in front of the building, step out of my car, and examine myself in the car window.

Red blouse with a plunging neckline, black pencil skirt, red lipstick. My long hair is flowing over my shoulders in a caramel cascade. I look soft, classy. I smile at myself, steel my nerves, and march into the bar.

It takes a minute for my eyes to adjust to the darkness inside, and I take in the room: cracked vinyl booths, tattered pool tables, a long bar up front with a neon Michelob sign above it.

I notice an old man with cloudy eyes and a rugged face staring at me. I'm startled for a minute. Is that him?

But he looks away, losing interest. I breathe a sigh of relief. It's not.

The bartender looks at me, and Nicholas isn't here.

What if he's really not who he was pretending to be, chickened out, and isn't coming? What if he's just some guy who wants to sext, but never really meet in person? I take another deep breath. I'm being stupid. He'll come. Of course he'll come.

I choose the cleanest table and take a seat, hanging my purse over the chair and primly crossing my high heels on the scuffed floor.

The bartender rounds the end of the bar, his damp towel sticking out of his back pocket, and approaches me.

"What can I get ya?" He eyes me, trying to decide what I'm here for. To pick up someone? To pick up anyone? Does he have a chance? I smile sweetly at him.

"Just a margarita. I'm meeting someone."

He nods and heads back to make my drink. I have to watch it. After not having lunch, I'll be a lightweight tonight.

It's okay. Drunk is good.

He's delivering my drink when the door opens, shining a sliver of sunlight onto the floor. I don't have to look to know it's Nicholas. I can feel it. It's almost like our energy is connected.

The bartender walks back to the bar, and I feel Nicholas walk to my table. I glance up through my eyelashes and study him for a second: expensive jeans and a crisp white button-down, tucked in. His hair is still damp, as though he's just taken a shower, and I want to inhale his clean man smell.

"Lindsey?" he asks, his voice low. Husky. Hearing my name on his lips shoots electricity down my spine.

"Hi." I smile up at him.

He smiles back at me, his teeth dazzlingly white.

"Can I sit?" he asks politely.

I nod again. "Feel free. As I said earlier, I probably won't bite."

I wink, and he smiles again.

21

Okay. This is good. It's good.

"I'll have a beer, Ryan," he calls to the barkeep. I like that he knows the bartender's name.

Ryan brings over an IPA, and I watch Nicholas tilt the cold beer bottle up and take a sip. He didn't ask for a glass. No pretense. I like him a little more.

"What can I get you guys to eat?" Ryan asks, hovering.

"Can I get a salad?" I glance up at him, and he barks out a laugh.

"Not on our menu, sweetheart. I can get you some celery, though. I have some for the wings."

Nicholas hides a grin, and I fight rolling my eyes.

"Perfect," I say good-naturedly. "Can I get that with ranch?"

Ryan does a double take because he'd been kidding, but he recovers. "Uh, yeah." He turns to Nicholas. "What about you? You want some garnish, too?"

He laughs as Nicholas answers, "Hardly. I'll have a cheeseburger."

"That's more like it," Ryan answers as he returns to the bar.

I take a gulp of my margarita and accidentally knock my purse off my chair. I heft it back up. It was my splurge last month. A pink checked Coach. It felt classy to me, and I couldn't help buying it.

Nicholas eyes it now, and then slides that gaze to my face.

I think I see amusement in his eyes. Why? Does it seem immature? I fight the flush that threatens my cheeks.

"It's nice to see you in person," he says quietly. "I'm glad you came."

This is real now. We're both sitting here, face-to-face. It should feel awkward, but it doesn't.

He glances down at his beer, and his fingers tighten around it. Uh-oh.

"Actually, I have to tell you something."

I feel the weight of a hammer getting ready to drop. Here it comes. I should've known someone as good as Nicholas has baggage. A kid? Two?

"I'm married," he says, grimacing.

The air leaves my belly in an audible *oomph*.

"Oh," I say, the word a sinking stone in a pond. *I should've known.*

He grimaces again.

"I know. I'm sorry," he says, and he sounds sincere, almost vulnerable, somehow.

"Then why are you here?" I manage to ask, taking another gulp of my margarita to hide my disappointment. I should've known he was too good to be true. I look down at his hand. How hadn't I noticed his ring earlier? I'd only been looking at the hand closest to me. I should've looked at the left.

His mossy eyes study me, shining even here in the dark room.

"I had to meet you," he finally says softly. "I've never done anything like this before. You just . . . you made me feel something. But I want to be upfront with you right now, at the beginning. And if you want to, you can leave. I'll walk you to your car, and that will be that."

"What a gentleman," I remark. He laughs, and the sound is honey in my ear, rich and thick.

"Chivalry isn't dead," he announces, and I concentrate on my drink, deciding what to say. Ryan delivers our food now, and purposely, I dunk a piece of celery in ranch and take a bite. Ryan rolls his eyes.

23

"Enjoy!" he tells us before leaving us alone.

We watch him retreat, and then Nicholas turns to me.

"Look," he says, before I can speak. "I didn't intend to meet someone, especially not someone like you. When we bumped into each other online, I never thought we'd take it any further. Then you started talking to me, and . . ."

He takes another drink and a steadying breath.

"You fascinate me," he says with an exhale. "And I sort of hate myself for being here, being selfish, but yet, here I am."

My heart picks up, pounding. Do I care that he's married? He can't be happy. Not if he's here, risking everything to see *me*.

That causes my belly to flutter.

His phone rings, and he glances at it. Then at me. He hesitates for the merest of milliseconds before picking it up.

"Hey." He answers and takes a sip of beer as he listens. "I stopped by BJ's. I figured no one would be home. Okay. I'll check on him. I'll see you after. Yep! Love you, too."

Love you, too. My stomach clenches a little, but his voice sounded wooden, not soft like he sounded when he was talking to me a minute ago. I don't like that he's telling someone else he loves her. Even if it's his wife. Oh my God, he has a wife. *What am I doing?*

"Everything okay?" I ask innocently, hiding my annoyance, my indecision.

"Yeah. Everyone is usually gone on Friday nights for football games. One son plays, and my daughter is a cheerleader. Tonight was an away game, but it got rained out, apparently. There's lightning."

"So, everyone is wondering where you are then?"

He chuckles. "Pretty much."

24

"Do you just have the two kids?"

He shakes his head. "No. An older son, too, who I actually have to call. He has hemophilia, and my wife can't reach him. I'm afraid I'll have to cut this evening short. I can't . . . I can't really talk to him while I sit here with you."

I want to hate him for stringing me along and not telling me he has three kids, let alone a wife. But he's so handsome and such a good dad. His wife must be an idiot not to keep someone like him happy. Doesn't she realize what crappy options are out there?

I realize in this moment that I don't care if he's married. If he doesn't, why should I? And who am I to make assumptions about a marriage I know nothing about?

I swear I see a flush on his cheek.

"I'm sorry. I just can't . . . sit here with you while I talk to him. I feel guilty enough already."

"How old is he?"

"Twenty-one."

"Oh my gosh," I exclaim. "You don't look nearly old enough to have a twenty-one-year-old son."

He flushes now.

"How old is your wife?" I ask, and immediately wish I hadn't been so nosy, but I feel a sudden innate competition, a need to draw a parallel now.

"Younger than me. By a couple of years. She's forty."

"Wow. She must've had him young," I point out.

"Nineteen. Just a baby." He doesn't appear fazed.

"Well, regardless, you look great," I say and lay my hand on his arm.

He coughs, just a little, and motions for Ryan, moving his arm away. It was discreet but purposeful. Damn.

"Can I get the check?" he asks and then glances at me. "For hers, too."

A surge of utter delight shoots through me. He *is* a gentleman.

I smile at him. "You don't need to do that." And before I can stop myself, I lean over and kiss him on the cheek. I inhale as I do. He smells good, like cedar, sunshine, and manliness.

He leans back ever so slightly. He had been still, allowing me to brush my lips across his skin. For one scant moment.

It was enough.

He stands up and pulls my seat out for me, still the gentleman. I grab my purse, and we head outside. As promised, he walks me to my car.

"I'd like to see you again," I tell him, looking up into his handsome face. His eyes instantly soften.

"Yeah?"

"Yeah."

"Okay. Then there's one other thing you should know."

I startle, and he shakes his head. "It's not bad. It's just . . . until I knew you would want to see me again . . . I mean, I couldn't take any chances . . . so I gave you my middle name."

"Nicholas isn't your name?"

He shakes his head.

"Then what is?"

"Ethan."

three

TESSA

My heart pounds, and my thoughts race. I struggle to swallow. There's a lump there that wasn't there before.

Holy shit.

This can't be happening.

I can't breathe as I stare at Ethan's iPad and scroll as far back through the messages as I can.

Her name is Lindsey, she's twenty-six, she's got caramel-colored hair and a fit, young body, and Ethan is sleeping with her.

My husband is having an affair.

I'll be in NY a couple more days, babe, he told her yesterday. *But you'll be the first thing I do when I get back!* ☺

Oh my God.

Oh my God.

He'd known he was planning on staying through this week-end. He'd known all along he wouldn't be spending it with me as we'd planned.

I exhale a long, shaky breath.

This isn't real.

He sounded so upset on the phone that this meeting had just "popped up" and that he couldn't come home. But he'd known. He didn't want to come home. How had he sounded so convincing? So normal?

Confusion dulls my senses, and I think I'm in physical shock. My mouth is dry, I can't swallow, and my hands shake so much I can't see the iPad straight.

He'd kissed me as he'd gotten into his truck to go to the airport. We'd made love right before that, and while it wasn't spectacular, everything was fine. Everything was normal. *I wish I didn't have to go*, he'd said.

But he'd lied. He's been lying.

My Ethan. Who is apparently not just mine.

My hands shake so badly that I drop the iPad and bound for the bathroom. I collapse in front of the toilet, heaving my guts up. As my stomach rebels, I can only think of one thing.

My husband cheated on me.

My heart is both numb and crushed. In denial and murderous. But above everything else, it's just broken.

I rest my cheek against the porcelain, wiping my mouth.

I look at the sink, the one we had picked out together; it's trough style, with farm faucets. He'd laughed when I wanted it but ultimately shrugged his shoulders. *Whatever you want, my love*, he'd said.

I *wanted* him to be faithful.

I had no idea that I had to worry about this.

How had I not known? He'd promised me—*It's me and you, babe. Me and you. 'Til death do us part.*

Oh my God. I jump to my feet and run back to the iPad, skimming the messages.

I'll be in NY a couple more days, babe.

He calls her *babe*, too. I stand still, and the room swirls around me, the wooden floors, the chandeliers, the lightning, the thunder, the rain. I stand frozen with my husband's traitorous words in my hands.

How could he do this to me? Does he love her? Have I been replaced?

I start to move, pacing as fast as my heart beats, like a wild animal. The more I move, the more I *feel* wild, like a beast unhinged. My thoughts come faster and faster, blurring together, and I can't swallow. My mouth is too dry, too hot, too clenched.

Fuck him. *Fuck him.*

I grab my phone from the charger, my logic flying out the window into the storm. Being tossed into the raging waves, along with my broken heart.

YOU MOTHERFUCKER, I text him. *I CAN'T BELIEVE YOU WOULD DO THIS.*

My fingers shake, and my legs can barely support me. My thoughts are red; my thoughts are rage.

There are three bubbles on my phone screen. Then he answers.

???

Question marks? Fucking question marks?

I dial his number; he answers, his voice is low and calm.

"Babe, I'm in a meeting right now. Is something wrong? Are you safe?"

"Am I fucking safe?" I hiss, like the wild animal I am. Fury slips between my teeth as I speak. "You are *fucking* cheating on me, you mother*fucking* bastard. What the hell did I ever do to deserve this?"

There's silence on his end, and I want to reach through the phone and choke his fucking throat.

"I've done everything for you. I've been everything you needed me to be," I say. My voice is ice, dripping down and shattering on the floor. "And *this* is how you repay me? You've ruined everything. The kids . . . Oh my God. The kids. Fuck you, Ethan."

"Babe," he starts, and I howl.

"Don't you ever call me that again! Not fucking ever again."

"Tessa," he says instead, ridiculously calm. "I'm in a meeting. But it's not what you think. I swear to God . . ."

"I saw with my own eyes, you *motherfucking* bastard. Do not sit there and lie to me. Do. Not. Lie. To. Me!"

"Tessa, I'll call you when I'm done here."

I never speak to anyone the way I just spoke to him, and he doesn't seem fazed. Calm, like a rock in stormy water. Fuck him.

I hang up on him and throw my phone across the room.

My emotions threaten to explode my body at the seams. My fury, blacker than the blackest night, mounts and grows and curls tight fingers around my heart and squeezes until I can't stand it any longer. I throw my head back, and I scream, shrieking as loud as I can, until my throat is hoarse. I'm as loud as the storm outside my windows. *I am the storm.*

Like an injured marathon runner crawling across the finish

line, I pull myself onto the couch, and I sit, like a stone statue, staring at Ethan's iPad, my hands on my knees.

The words. Jesus. They blur, then focus, blur then focus.

Lindsey Vale.

Lindsey fucking Vale.

I need answers. I need to see this woman—the face, the body, the legs, the eyes of the woman who has stolen my husband. I need to know what she has that I don't. I need to see her in person. And I need it all right now.

Right. Fucking. Now.

I pick up the iPad and a wave of icy calmness descends upon me.

Hey babe, I type, acting like Ethan. *I got home early, and I'm at home alone. Wanna come ride out the storm with me?* ☺

I'm breathing in pants now, because I don't know what I'm doing, but my fingers are doing it anyway, typing out words with consequences that I don't yet understand. Lindsey Vale answers immediately.

OMG you're home?? But risking my life in THIS?

For a split second, I feel relieved, already thinking about what else to do, how else to get answers from her, when she answers again.

C U soon.

She doesn't ask where his wife is, doesn't ask any questions at all. She simply says she'll come see my husband in a dangerous, raging storm.

I'm stunned as I stare at the words, and I quickly delete them before Ethan sees them on his phone and ruins everything. This may be the only chance I have to get the truth before Ethan has time to cover up his tracks.

I stare at her name on the iPad, and then her words.

C U soon.

My husband's lover is coming to my house. Right now.

What do I do?

A plan, jagged and rough, begins to form in my foggy mind, and I lunge into action.

I sprint to the bedroom, change into a good shirt and jeans that accentuate my ass, and pull my hair back into a chic bun. She's not going to think she's better than me just because she's younger.

I dash out again. My temper is an all-consuming fire, raging inside my brain, and I can't remember one moment to the next.

I think of the pictures of her. Lindsey. She's on her way here, and I'm going to get some answers about a problem I didn't even know I fucking had.

My husband is sleeping with this woman. He's sleeping with us both. My husband. The man I trusted with my heart and my life.

My Ethan.

Mine.

Goddamnit.

I pick up my wineglass and hurl it into the fireplace, where it shatters into a million jagged shards. I stare at them, and as I do, the power abruptly goes out. It didn't even flicker in warning.

But now . . . now . . . I welcome the darkness. It's as black as my heart. Bad things can hide in the night, and in this moment, the goodness has been sucked from me, all the marrow pulled from my bones, and replaced with a deep, seething hatred.

I'm a lioness hiding in the darkness, waiting. Stalking.

I grab a flashlight and go from room to room, lighting candles. I pause in the foyer, grabbing a piece of paper. I scribble on it, as close to Ethan's handwriting as I can make it.

Bedroom, I write. A smile stretches across my face as my plan forms. She's going to regret crossing me. She and Ethan both.

I rush to the bedroom and dig through Ethan's top drawers. I know they're in here . . . There they are. I triumphantly pull out the handcuffs I'd given him last Valentine's Day, remembering how we'd put them to good use.

I wonder if he'd seen this girl that night, too. When he said he got called away for a job site emergency, had he gone to see her? I'm so fucking dumb.

The inky red rage clouds the edges of my vision, and I toss the handcuffs onto the middle of the bed and scribble another note.

Handcuff yourself to the headboard, both ankles and one hand.

I hear my phone ringing in the kitchen. I know it's Ethan, but I don't care.

In this moment, I hate him. If he were here, I'd punch him in the face, smash his goddamn balls, and then push him off the balcony. I'd . . . I don't even know what else I'd do, but I don't need to know because he's not here.

But Lindsey will be.

I try to imagine the look on her face when she sees me instead of my husband. Will she be furious? Will she be afraid?

She should be.

I can't stop the odd smile that my mouth contorts into, and for a moment, I'm scared of myself.

What have I just done?

What am I going to do?

Lightning cracks outside, and I see it flash in the small gap at the bottom of the shutters. All hell is breaking loose out there.

In here, too.

Like a predator, I creep out of the bedroom and wait in the shadows until the door opens a few minutes later.

four

LINDSEY

I'm coming in from a jog when Ethan finally texts. It has been two days since our date, and I was starting to think he wasn't interested after all.

My hands are sweaty as I grab my phone.

Hi! How's your day going?

I smile. It almost feels like the bumbling efforts of a teenager, like he wants to talk to me but doesn't know how. I'm sure it's because he's married and he's never done something like this before. Maybe it took him two days to work up the courage to contact me again.

Honestly, it's sweet.

I was just out running. Thinking about you, I answer.

There are three immediate bubbles. He's typing something.

What were you thinking?

I pause.

Should I tell him I've been obsessing over him all day? Wondering if I'm important enough to him that he'll risk his marriage to see me again? The fact that he gives me a strange feeling of power.

My finger twitches.

Of course I shouldn't say that. I don't ever want to remind him of his marriage.

That you intrigue me.

I was thinking about his green eyes and that flash of electricity that had bound me to my seat. The heat that had flooded me when he smiled at me. I was thinking about all of it.

The feeling is mutual, trust me, he answers. *Are you on Facebook? I tried to find you, but no luck.*

Hmmm. Stalking me?

He sends a crying laughing emoji.

Um, no. I just wanted to learn more about you. And I wanted to see your face.

I take a quick selfie and send it. *Here you go. Now you can see it whenever you want. And no. I'm not on Facebook. I'm on Instagram, though.*

That's a lie. Of course I'm on Facebook, but that's where I share pictures of my son. I don't want him to see those yet.

If he's asking about it, though, *he* must be on Facebook. I open my laptop and look. I plug Ethan's name in and find him right away.

I see you! I tell him. *On Facebook.*

Oh yeah? What do you see?

I skim through his posts, through his pictures. He's successful. He's been tagged in a few posts about award-winning building designs. Some of his pictures are of him in black tie at events and even galas. Rich people stuff.

Hmmm, I answer. *You seem like a handsome guy who has it all figured out.*

He answers immediately.

Well, appearances can be deceiving.

How so? I answer.

Never mind, he cops out. *People are just usually different than others think.*

Are you? I ask boldly.

Maybe. I don't really know.

I look through his profile again. There are pictures of him on a sailboat, and his arm is slung around the shoulders of a beautiful woman, slender and tall. Happy kids smile in the background. They look like a Kennedy family, for fuck's sake.

Well, it looks like you're a guy who loves the outdoors, his kids, and his wife. Is that true?

For some reason, I find myself holding my breath until he answers.

Yes.

I don't know what I expected, but that one stark word stabs me in the heart. If he loves his wife, why is he talking to me? Before I can reply, he sends another.

Do you ever feel, though, that there's more to you than anyone knows? Maybe even more than you know yourself?

My heart pounds. This man intrigues me. Everything about him. He seems to have the perfect life. Is that a lie, though?

Do you feel like there's more to life than you see? I ask him. *Because I do. I see everything that other people have . . . nice things, love, a perfect life, and I'm envious.*

His answer is immediate. *No one has a perfect life.*

Not even you? I ask. It's pathetic, fishing, but I ask it anyway.

Not even me.

I don't know what to say to that. What I do know is that I want to keep talking to him, but I'm afraid anything I say could scare him away. He's married. He knows not to tempt himself with someone like me. His wife should have made that clear to him somewhere along the way.

I look at his picture again. Those hands. What I wouldn't give to have them on me.

You're very, very good-looking.

There's no reply, and I feel that I've pushed too far.

Damn it.

I wait, but there's nothing. I sigh and go take a shower. When I emerge, toweling off my hair, his answer is waiting for me.

Thank you. You are, too.

He's interested.

He doesn't know how to proceed, and honestly, I don't either. I answer with a winky face and leave it be for now. I can't appear too needy or persistent.

Instead of continuing the conversation, I google his wife.

Her name is Tessa. She has brown eyes and blond hair. She's pretty, and her smile seems glamorous. But she's got one thing I happily don't: age. She doesn't look all that old, maybe mid-thirties, but she must act it. She would never be able to keep up with *me*.

I scour her profile and discover that she's a businesswoman. Holy shit. I narrow my eyes. She owns Blush. I buy my makeup there, when I can afford it.

Surely that's not right. But after a quick search, I find that it is, in fact, correct.

Tessa Taylor owns Blush. And she's married to Ethan. How do I compete with that? Until I finish college, I'm just a secretary. Even then, even after I have my nursing degree, it's still modest in comparison.

I try to force that thought out of my mind. I don't have to be compared to her, and I don't have to compete with her.

Ethan isn't interested in me for what I do. He's interested in me for who I am. What I look like. If he wasn't, he wouldn't be talking to me.

Besides, businesswomen are brisk and cold, aren't they?

I click on her pictures and look at her children. Three older teenagers, all good-looking, like their parents. The middle one looks like Ethan, with the same hazel eyes. I'm only a decade older than them, but I could be a good stepmother. I know I could. The kids seem well-behaved. But I'm getting ahead of myself, as I always do. My mom always says I'm too impulsive.

As the minutes tick past, though, I get even more curious. I google their address, and to my surprise, I find it rather easily.

It's in a nice area in Santa Rosa Beach, right on the shoreline. I don't think there are any homes there for under one mil.

I grab my car keys. I want to see it in person.

The Florida sun shines bright as I drive the winding roads to their home, and the mailboxes grow farther and farther apart, separated by lush palm trees. I look for Ethan's address.

As I expected, it's a very nice home, breathtaking even. Its Spanish-tiled roof and gabled peaks poke through the trees, but it's far enough back from the main road that I can't see it clearly.

I want to stop and examine it, but there aren't any places to pull off the road without being obvious.

With a sigh, I resort to turning around down the road and driving slowly back past the house.

I can't begin to imagine what it must be like to live here. But I'd like to.

I think about it long after I've gotten home, long after I've done my laundry and my homework.

It's when I'm lying in bed that I hear my phone again. My

arm slinks from beneath the covers, and my eyes widen when I see it's Ethan.

I look at the clock. It's midnight.

Are you still up?

I wait for a few minutes to answer.

I am now. ☺

Oh, sorry. I didn't mean to wake you.

No worries. What's up?

I just wondered . . . if you're thinking about me as much as I'm thinking about you.

Yes, I answer. *I am.*
It feels good to be so blunt, so honest.
He answers back, *Good.*
It gives me the balls to ask him a question of my own. *Were you hoping I would be?*
My heart beats once, then there's an answer.

Yes.

Adrenaline starts to pulse through my veins, and I'm so excited I can barely stand it. I hadn't misread the signals. He is into me.

I guess that makes me a terrible person, he adds.

Why?

Because I'm married, and I'm talking to a beautiful woman right now, he replies.

He thinks I'm beautiful. My heart glows.

That only makes you human, I tell him. *What are you doing now?*

> *Everyone else is asleep. My son is having an issue so my wife had to leave to go tend to him.*

> *Is he okay?*

> *He let himself run out of his meds. It was stupid. He knows without them, he could die if he gets even a tiny cut.*

OMG. I'm so sorry, I answer. *That must be so hard.*

I've learned about the blood disorder in school, of course. I know it can be very serious. Ethan is definitely not exaggerating that Colt could die from even a small cut, if he's not medicated.

> *It IS hard. Tessa's making it harder, though. She's having a hard time letting him go. He went away for college, and she lives in fear that something is going to happen to him.*

She'll get used to it, I answer.

You'd think, he agrees. *But not yet. She spends more time worrying about him than anything else. Well, other than work.*

There's resentment there. I can feel it. I pounce on it.

I'm sure she pays attention to you, too, I tell him. *You're very important to her, too.*

It certainly doesn't feel like it.

And there it is. He feels neglected.

Have you tried telling her your feelings? I ask it innocently, as though I actually want to help.

Oh yes. We've had numerous discussions.

Hmm. I'm sorry. I'm not sorry.

> *It's just one of those situations. She's got tunnel vision when it comes to Colt. She feels guilty that he was born with this, even though it wasn't her fault. She lives in fear that he'll die.*

> *That sounds terrible. For you, and for her.*

> *Yeah, it is.*

So are you in bed alone? I ask, changing the subject, tired of talking about his wife and his problems at home. I need to distract him from that. I might as well make the first move.

Yes, why?

Are you thinking about me?

My heart pounds against my ribcage, the bones the only thing holding it back from bursting through my skin. This could totally turn him away. It might be too assertive. It might scare him.

Yes. That's why I texted. ☺

I exhale, long and slow. My fingers fly over the keys.

What were you thinking?

I was wondering why a young girl like you would want to see an old guy like me.

You're only 43, I tell him. *That's not old. And I'm not a girl. I'm all woman.*

To prove it, I take a picture of my bare breasts and send it.

There's no answer.

Then there's three bubbles.

Then they disappear.

Stunned speechless? I ask.

I'm joking, but I know this is a pivotal moment. Wanting to meet me for dinner was one thing. Even texting me in the middle of the night was one thing. But to accept a nude picture from someone other than his wife is something else altogether.

It's crossing a clear line. This moment could change everything. I wait, holding my breath.

You're so beautiful.

five

TESSA

My rage is almost too much to contain. I'm a shell of myself, and something more powerful has taken over. Something primitive and primal that comes from the reptilian part of my brain, something without logic or reason.

The woman opening my front door thought she could steal my life.

What gives her the right?

I sharpen my claws against the wall.

What made her think she could?

Poised at the edge of the foyer, I hear her high heels tap across my stone floor.

What part did my husband play?

My heart quickens, and my rage flows freely in my veins.

Why wasn't I enough?

Answers are within my grasp. I feel them within my fingers, and I will get every last one of them.

What will I do to her?

I hear soft breaths as she opens the envelope I left for her on the entry table, the rustle of paper. The note simply says *Bedroom*.

She's good at following instructions—she immediately makes her way down the hallway and opens my bedroom door.

On the posh gray duvet I picked out with Ethan last year, there is another note. *Handcuff yourself to the bed, both ankles and one hand.*

The scrawled writing must fool her, because she giggles and then crawls onto my bed, the bed I share with my husband.

I hear the clink of the handcuffs, and I don't trust myself. My breaths are ragged, and my legs quake. Should I even go in? Should I walk away?

The wind howls outside, and I know that's not a real option. I can't go out in that.

For better or for worse, my husband's mistress and I are both here for the duration of the storm.

"I'm ready," she calls out, and then she giggles again, because she thinks she is preparing to see Ethan. She sounds so young, so stupid. So naïve.

I take a deep breath and lean on the wall for just one moment. I need answers, and she can give them to me. I didn't get to where I am in life by being a pushover.

She tried to take what is mine.

I throw my shoulders back and stick my chin out.

I stride into the room, and she startles, spread-eagle in the middle of my bed. She's pretty, with her long hair and her big brown eyes and her twenty-six-year-old legs. But I knew that already. I saw the pictures.

"Who are you?" she demands, struggling against the cuffs, but it's too late. She's restrained, and I have the keys.

"I'm Ethan's wife," I tell her calmly, sitting on the foot of the bed. "And you're Lindsey."

"I didn't know he was married," she stutters, and I ponder her acting skills. If I didn't know better, I'd believe her.

"Yes, you did," I answer. I study her. "I saw the texts."

She freezes, and she studies me, her eyes darting to the door and back. Looking for Ethan?

"He's not coming," I tell her calmly. "He's out of town for the weekend."

"He's back." Lindsey shakes her head. "He asked me to come wait the storm out with him."

"Here? In *my* home?" I laugh, and it's bitter. "I wonder . . . did those texts come from *this*?"

I hold up Ethan's iPad.

Lindsey stares at me, doe-eyed. In this moment, she almost looks like a child. A *conniving* child, but a child nonetheless. She thought she had so much power, sneaking around to steal my husband. She had no idea who she was dealing with.

"It was you?" I watch as understanding settles into the depths of her eyes, like a fog rolling in over a city. "Why would you do that?"

It's my turn to chuckle now. "That's a stupid question, Lindsey. Because you're fucking my husband and I want to know everything."

"Nothing has been going on," she says defiantly as she lies to my face.

"You're lying," I tell her. *How am I so calm?* It's like my rage has settled into ice, freezing even my lungs. I don't know how I'm still standing, still breathing. It feels as if my bones could shatter from the cold.

Lindsey sucks in a breath, and her free hand clenches into a fist. "You don't know what you're talking about."

"Please don't insult my intelligence, you *whore*." I rarely call names. Rarely even think them. I'm usually much more controlled. But not tonight.

Now that's all I can think when I see her. Obscenities. Giant red words.

"I found the texts. I know what you are. I know what you've been doing. Both of you."

Anger tints my words, and I pause to regain my composure. I have to be calm. I have to be collected. *She* can't affect me. My shaking hands betray my will, though.

I'm stronger than she is, I remind myself. I'm not controlled by whim or fancy. I am a mature adult.

She waits, her brown eyes wary, and a delicate bead of sweat rolls down her forehead.

"You deserve to pay for that," I continue steadily.

"What are you going to do?"

"I'm not sure yet. I guess we'll figure that out as we go."

"I'll scream," she threatens, and I laugh.

"No one will hear you. My kids are gone. There's a hurricane outside. Scream all you want."

She does, and I scream with her. I throw my head back and shriek, a deranged wolf.

She stops and stares at me, fear swimming in her eyes, because she thinks I'm crazy. I smile.

"Lindsey? Do you think I've snapped, like those stories on the news about temporary insanity? Well, guess what? *I have.*"

She screams again, terrified this time. I don't want to hear it. It's loud and panicked, a banshee in desperate need of fresh souls. I walk out.

I pause at the door, though, cocking my head.

"Oh, and Lindsey?" She looks at me. "Ethan fucked me on those sheets before he left."

She starts up again. I walk toward the kitchen, sitting at the table while I wait for her to exhaust herself.

As I sit, I try texting my husband again.

Tell me everything.

How did it start?

Why?

Why would you do this to me?

He doesn't answer, and then I see why. Each text has a red exclamation point next it, bounced back as undeliverable.

No service.

The freaking storm.

Son of a bitch.

I'm stuck here without cell service. Of all the times in the world, why now when I *need* to hear from my husband?

I march to Ethan's study and look for the last phone bill. I scan it, and find that 1,014 of his nearly 2,000 text messages last month had been to Lindsey's number. Over half went to her. The rest were divided between our kids, me, and his job.

I'm stunned as I sit in his leather chair, the storm wailing behind me and the wind rattling the storm shutters.

How did I not see this happening?

I look at the phone calls. Numerous calls back and forth between the two of them, often in the evening hours when he was here at home, even some in the night when he was supposed to be in bed sleeping next to me. Had he snuck down to his office to call her? Had he hidden in the bathroom behind the closed door?

How had I not seen this?

I'm so stupid. So, so oblivious.

None of this feels real, except for the screaming from down the hall. The voice gets thinner and hoarser, until finally, thirty minutes later, it gives out.

I take her a glass of ice-cold water, because even though I'm furious, I'm not stupid. If she loses her voice, she can't give me answers.

I hold the cup to Lindsey's lips, and she drinks. Then she grabs me with her free hand, her nails digging into my arm. She's stronger than she looks, and she tries to wrestle me onto the bed.

I wrench away as red-hot scratches are gashed into my skin, and I toss the rest of the ice water into her face.

Lindsey is sputtering on the bed, water dripping down her neck, as I stare at her.

"Really?" I ask her. "You're handcuffed. You *can't* get the upper hand."

To make sure of that, I grab one of Ethan's ties and yank her free hand up to the headboard, tying it tight. She can't grab me again.

I stand in satisfaction above her, trying to catch my breath as I ignore the sting of her scratches. Blood forms in a jagged line down my forearm, and now my skin is under her fingernails. Damn it.

I am panting as I realize that I could go to jail for this. I could lose my kids, my job, my life as I know it.

I should stop.

But she stares at me, and those lips have been on Ethan. Those hands have touched him. He has been inside of her.

My blood feels as though it's exploding inside my body, too hot, too furious to be contained. My pulse pounds into my palms, and I clench my hands tight. Lindsey goes still.

"Are you going to kill me?" she asks, her voice quiet. She's afraid, and that gives me satisfaction.

"I don't know," I tell her honestly. "I want answers. I want to see you regret what you did. I don't necessarily want to go to jail."

She bursts out laughing. "You're holding me here against my will. You're going to jail."

I level a gaze at her. Her eye makeup is smeared. Her façade is already breaking. She's not so perfect now.

"You let yourself into my house," I remind her. "You climbed on top of my bed and *you* restrained *your*self. You came here willingly."

"I'm not willing now," she spits, twisting against her restraints.

"Too late."

I sit down on the bed again, and I rest my elbow on her newly shaven leg. She thought she'd have them wrapped around my husband's hips by now, I'm sure. She kicks at me, and I move away.

"Answer my questions, and we'll see how it goes," I tell her. "Tell me the truth. Don't even think about lying."

"Why don't you ask your husband," she suggests, her voice harsh.

"I don't have a signal, and he's in New York. You're here, though." I stare at her, my gaze hard and unflinching. "How did you meet? How did it start?"

She turns her face away, purposely not looking at me, refusing to answer. I sigh.

"It'll go better for you if you cooperate," I say. "I'm not in a *healthy* mindset right now."

"Fuck you," she spits.

"Listen, you little whore. I've spent my entire adult life with that man. We've weathered so many storms I can't even count them all. And you think you can just waltz in and take it all?"

"I'm not answering your questions. He loves me. He wants to be with me. I'll let him tell you what he wants to tell you. But I won't mess up anything for the divorce."

I burst out laughing now, at the absolute trust in my husband on her face.

"You realize that he cheated on me, a woman he's known for his entire adult life. What makes you think he'd leave me for you? That he'd abandon our entire life . . . for you?"

I stare down at her, condescending, but I can't help it.

"I didn't mean to hurt you," she tries. "This was never about you."

"Of course it was," I snap. "He's my husband. It's all about me."

"I just . . . I love Ethan," she says, softer now. "I wasn't thinking about you at all. I should've, I'm sorry."

I ignore her because she's not sorry.

Yet.

six

LINDSEY

God, this week passed slowly.

Ethan's good morning texts helped the time pass, though. Every morning, without fail, he texted me on his way to work, wishing me a good day.

I started each day out with a smile and a joyous, hopeful feeling in my heart. I mean, who does that in this day and age? Who is that thoughtful?

I'm lucky to have met him. I can't blow it now.

I stand in front of my closet and sift through my clothes. I ignore the stacks of nursing scrubs I have to wear during my clinical rotations and focus instead on the fancier clothes I wear for my day job.

I decide upon a black silk wrap blouse with a bow in the front, and a black-and-pink-flowered pencil skirt. Both items accentuate my curves without looking slutty. In fact, they make me look professional, intelligent, ambitious. They're both Anne

Klein, both something I wear to work to feel pretty. Someday, I'll be able to afford Armani.

I'm laying the outfit on my bed when the phone rings.

It's my son.

I pick up, and Logan's voice is quiet, sullen.

"Mommy, you were supposed to call me tonight."

Shit. I was. I was so preoccupied with Ethan that I forgot.

"Oh, baby, I'm sorry! Work was so busy, and I just now walked through the door. Tell me about your day, though!"

He gets over being mad quickly and tells me about his little friend Clive, who ate a cricket for five dollars.

"It wasn't your five dollars, was it?" I ask.

"No. I don't got no money," he replies.

"I don't *have* any money," I correct.

"That's what I said. Gramma says you probably won't come get me like you said," he says now. He's wary, suspicious. I've broken promises before, but I've always had a reason. I want him to think I'm good. I try to be, but I just don't have the money.

"She's wrong," I tell him. "I promised you I would come get you this summer and bring you here. I'm working hard to save money for that."

"Pinkie promise?" he asks, hopeful.

My heart twinges. I don't know if I'll be able to or not. Childcare is outrageous. I work full-time and go to school every evening. That's a *lot* of childcare expenses. Once I finish school and I'm making more money, absolutely. But I can't disappoint him now. Not today.

"Yes," I tell him. "I do."

"When will it be?" he asks me, excited now.

I count. "Well, this is October. But school will be out before you know it, sweetie. I've got a two-bedroom apartment. You'll have your own room, and there's a pond where we can feed the ducks!"

"I can't wait!" he sings, chattering now.

I'm a sorry excuse for a mother, and I feel so bad for Logan that he got stuck with me. Out of all the mothers in the world, he got me.

He talks until I hear my mother in the background, calling for him to take a bath and get ready for bed. He mumbles good-night to me, and then my mother is on.

"He got an A on that big spelling test he was worried about," my mother tells me coolly. "Did you remember to even ask him about it?"

Fuck.

"I thought not," she continues. "Talking to him so sporadically only hurts him and makes it harder on me. He acts out for two days afterward. Either call him regularly, or . . ."

"Or don't call at all?" I ask softly.

My mother is quiet.

"I came here to make a better life for myself," I tell her. "You know that. I don't know why you try to make me feel guilty about that."

"You didn't have to go across the country for that," my mother points out. "You could've gone to school in Phoenix. I could've helped take care of Logan. You wouldn't have had to leave him behind."

"I had to get a fresh start." I'm adamant, because it's a conversation we've had a dozen times before. If she hasn't understood yet, she's never going to. "It's only temporary. And I didn't get a scholarship in Phoenix. I got a scholarship *here*."

My mother sighs. "I'm only saying . . . do what is best for him. Figure something out. Be present for him."

She hangs up, and I'm left alone in my tiny apartment.

Guilt bubbles up in me, like dark clouds. I'm too selfish. I wanted to get away from the demons of my past, from my ex, from my mother . . . but I didn't want to get away from my kid.

Not really.

Did I? Had I left my mom to take care of Logan—to sit with him when he's sick or throwing tantrums or bouncing off the walls from being hyper—simply because I didn't have the patience? Were my excuses about not having enough money all a lie? I mean, I didn't try super hard to get scholarships in Phoenix. I tried to get them here. Far from my mother.

Damn it. I've allowed her to get under my skin.

I'm not a bad person.

I look at the pink-and-black pencil skirt I'm wearing tonight. I'd just splurged on it last week. I should've saved the money instead. But it had fit me so perfectly, hugging my hips yet making me look classy.

I should've put the money in the bank.

I shove the troubling thoughts away. It's a problem for another day.

Tonight, Ethan is coming over.

I take pains getting ready, making sure my makeup is perfect. I wear a nude lipstick. I don't want to look like a clown with red lipstick smeared all over my face after he kisses me.

I am buffed, polished, perfumed, and ready within the hour. And Ethan is right on time.

There is a knock on my door at precisely 7:00 p.m. I take a deep, calming breath, then answer it with a glowing smile.

Ethan stands in front of me, breathtakingly handsome, the perfect combination of manicured and manly in his well-fitting slacks and his crisp white button-down. He smiles at me.

"Am I early?"

He hands me flowers, and my heart flutters. He's already seen my bare breasts. Why am I so nervous?

"No, you're right on time. Come in."

As he walks past me, I catch a whiff of his cologne, subtle and mossy. It reminds me of the color of his eyes. A forest on an autumn day. Being with him makes me feel emotions I didn't know I had come to life inside of me. It's exhilarating.

"Would you like a drink?" I ask, and he flashes me a grin.

"Sure."

"Please, sit. Get comfortable," I tell him as I bustle into the kitchen. I get him a bottle of the IPA he ordered at BJ's and myself a glass of wine. I pour it behind the refrigerator door so he doesn't see how cheap it is.

I kick the door closed with my foot, my hands full of alcohol. I carefully hand him his, and then I curl up next to him on the sofa.

"You smell nice," he tells me, so politely.

"Thank you." I take a ladylike sip of wine.

I itch to get closer to him, to put my hand on his knee, to stroke his fingers. But I have to pace myself. I level a gaze at him.

"How was your week?"

He takes a gulp of beer.

"That good?" I chuckle. He laughs.

"It was fine. I kept thinking about this night. And then I felt guilty about that. But then I'd think about it again. And again."

My heart thunders, and I worry he might hear it.

"I was looking forward to it, too," I admit.

Ethan moves toward me, and I think he's going to caress my hair. I lean toward him, but he reaches around me and retrieves my hot pink stethoscope from the end table.

He startles when I lean in, and I yank back, cheeks flushed.

He ignores the awkward moment, holding up my stethoscope.

"Have you been playing doctor?" He smiles.

I shake my head. "Nursing school. But we can play doctor if you want." Now he's the one blushing.

"My sister is a nurse," he says. "She went back and got her BSN. I respect the hell out of nurses. Long hours, ungrateful patients. It's a tough job."

When he looks at me now, I see respect in his eyes. I bask in it.

"Whenever Colt has to be hospitalized, it's always the nurses who make the difference," he says. "Good nurses can make the entire experience tolerable."

"I'll remember that," I answer, "and try to do the same."

He nods with a smile. "Then you'll go far."

God. I ache to please him, long for praise from him.

"Hey, about the other night," I say, flushing. I don't want him to think I'm easy, but I also don't want to push him away. "I was alone, and I like you, and I might've gotten carried away. With the picture. I hope you don't think less of me."

Ethan's head snaps up, and he honestly seems startled.

"No. It was . . . I mean . . . it was nice to have someone interested in me like that," he finally settles on. "You have no idea."

How could his wife not want this beautiful man?

"Okay, good," I say softly. "I just don't want to mess this up."

"You won't." His voice is gentle, and his eyes are on mine, unwavering. "Can I kiss you?"

I nod. He cups my face in his big hands, and his lips lower to mine. They're soft yet firm, exactly right. The kiss takes my breath away, and when he pulls back, he seems flustered.

"You're so beautiful," he tells me, his arm around my shoulders. I can smell him, and it's intoxicating.

"Thank you," I murmur. He tucks a loose tendril of hair behind my ear.

"I don't know what I did to deserve this," he says, and he sounds half-regretful. "But I'm probably going to hell."

I squirm against him, eager and ready and suddenly unafraid to let him know it.

"Then we'll have to make it worth it."

He leans back into me, but after a few minutes, he pulls away. Abruptly.

"I'm sorry," he says, embarrassed. "I just . . . Can we slow down a little? This is the first time I've . . . Well, I just want to wrap my head around it."

"Of course," I tell him. I sound so understanding, even though I'm annoyed he isn't ready to cross that final line yet. "We can go as slowly as you like, Ethan. This is new for me, too."

I stroke his back, and he hugs me tight.

It's okay, I tell myself. *It's okay.* My endgame is still in sight. Good things come to those who wait.

seven

TESSA

Lindsey has a temper.

I linger outside the door, listening to her thrash on the bed. She practically growls, furious and completely oblivious to any part she's played in getting here.

"You realize you're here because you chose to be, right?" I ask her curiously as I enter the room. "You chose to come here, thinking you were meeting my husband. You handcuffed yourself to my bed. If I let you go, it's because I'm a good person. I don't think most women would."

"Most women wouldn't be doing this," she snaps, and she's got piss in her hair somehow. She reeks of it. "You're a fucking psycho."

"*I* am?" I ask incredulously, and the odor in the room is unmistakable. "Did you pee my bed?"

She's quiet now and looks away. Even in the candlelight, I can see the giant urine spot she's lying on. I suck in a breath. A woman peed herself because of me. I pause for a moment, then another.

What kind of monster am I?

She looks slowly back at me.

"Ethan loves me," she announces, and my heart is steel again.

"Did he tell you that?"

She's silent again.

"You found out who I am and how much money we have, and you went after him, didn't you?" I ask. I clench the footrail of the bed hard. The acrid scent of urine is heavy in the air, and I want to bury my nose in my shirt. I'll have to burn this mattress.

"That's not true," she says, willing to at least say that much. "I had no idea at first. I didn't even know he was married."

"So you say." I'm dubious. "But Ethan wouldn't just do this. Not without being tempted. I know him. I've known him for so long."

"Clearly you don't know him well enough," she points out, and the rage threatens to overtake me again, because she's right. I didn't see this coming.

As I look at the urine-soaked girl on my bed, I have a million thoughts. What will I tell my friends . . . my colleagues . . . my kids . . . my parents? They're all going to know he was willing to risk losing me for *this*.

"You know he wouldn't divorce me for you, right? If he wanted to, he'd have done it already. He just wanted to have his cake and eat it, too."

I act as calmly as I can, belying my racing heart. That last part has to be true. It's the most rational thing I can think of. If she really meant anything to him, he would've left me for her, right?

But he didn't. So she means nothing.

Please, God.

I look down at her cheap shoes, one heel wedged into my mattress.

"You say you love him, but you don't know him. You don't know anything about the boy he was or how we grew up together. You never knew him when he was building himself."

"So?" Lindsey rolls her eyes. "None of that matters now."

"But it does. That stuff is what creates a person."

I watch Lindsey as she lies limply on the bed. She's not struggling now. "You're nothing," I point out. "You're still being formed. I remember those days . . . but I don't think you have a dream or a goal. We're different, you and I. I always had a goal, something to work for. And of course, I always had Ethan."

She glares at me, looking like a Sunday-morning walk of shame.

"You don't have Ethan," she says, her voice as thin as ice. "If you truly did, he never would've given me a second glance. But it was so easy, Tessa. All I had to do was text him. After that, he was mine."

I ignore her, but tumultuous feelings storm in my belly, old wooden ships of emotion that I desperately want to sink.

"We used to eat canned soup and ramen," I say, thinking back to the days right after college. "We could only afford the water or the electricity, never both, so one was always over-due. We were constantly robbing Peter to pay Paul and hiding from the landlord when he came to collect rent. It felt so hard, so stressful. But we learned so much. Through adversity comes strength, you know. And Ethan and I learned it together. We've weathered storms you can only imagine."

"Life shouldn't be all about weathering storms," Lindsey tells me, so knowingly, yet so naïve. "I know about Colt. How you're so focused on him, then the other kids, and then your business . . . that there's nothing left for Ethan at the end of every day. Marriage shouldn't be like that, Tessa. You failed him."

My heart seems to stop.

Ethan discussed Colton with this girl? My precious, beautiful Colt? *With her?*

I look at her, trying desperately to hide my confusion and pain. But she sees it right away, and her eyes light up.

"Oh, you didn't know?" She pauses, and I'm stunned speechless. "He told me everything. I'm his confidante, everything you stopped being to him, Tessa. If you think about it, everything that has happened is your fault. You stopped being a wife."

I think of the endless sleepless nights I've spent over the years worrying about Colt. How Ethan has always been there for me. We've worried together. Of course we have. Our kids are everything to us, all three of them.

This woman is lying.

Obviously, Ethan talked about it with her, but he wouldn't say bad things about me, or about Colt.

"When all you do is weather storms, it's time to end the relationship. Face it, Tessa. And for the record, you don't know anything about me. I'm in college; I have goals. I'm going to have a great life, and Ethan is going to be a big part of it."

Her voice is bile, each word concentrated with it. I can't take it. I can't take her arrogance. I pull my phone out of my pocket, searching through my videos for one from our last trip.

Lindsey stares at me from our king-sized bed. Its broad vastness makes her look even smaller. I ignore her skinniness, her dewy youth, and I turn my phone toward her.

"I have something to show you," I tell her. "I hope you don't mind."

She rolls her eyes, trying to maintain her disdain. She's not composed. I smile, then press Play.

On the screen is a luxurious hotel room in the tropics. I stood on the balcony earlier this year, filming my shirtless, handsome husband while he got ready for dinner.

He reached for a white button-down shirt. "You want me to wear this one, right?" he asked with a grin. I nodded, and the camera jiggled. I loved him in that shirt.

"You look so sexy in that one," I told him.

He waggled his eyebrows. "I *am* sexy. Just ask me, I'll tell you."

I giggled, and he buttoned his shirt up, leaving the top three casually undone, and rolled up the sleeves.

"I love you, you know that?" he asked. "This trip was a good idea."

"I know," I agreed.

"It's too easy to take each other for granted," he said, running a hand through his hair. "We need stuff like this to remind us."

On the screen, I saw my hand slide up Ethan's chest, and I could hear his phone buzzing.

"Someone is really trying to get ahold of you," I told him. He winced.

"It's just work. I swear, you'd think they can't get through a day without me."

"Well, I know *I* can't," I said, my voice velvety.

Ethan grinned. "You want more of this?" he gestured toward his groin, and we laughed. He pulled me close. My hand had fallen to my side, so the picture on the screen is blurred now, a close-up of his gray linen pants.

There is still sound, however, and Lindsey and I can hear it loud and clear.

"Let's skip dinner," Ethan growled, and I remember his lips were against my neck. "I want you."

"You always want me," I said. "You're shameless."

"I'm in love with my wife," he countered.

His phone buzzed again.

"Maybe you'd better get that," I suggested.

"It's no one important," he answered. "I've got everything that matters right here."

I press Pause and turn to Lindsey, because I know something now. I feel it in my gut.

"You were the one calling, weren't you?" I ask now. Her face is pale, but her eyes are cold. "He said it was work, but it didn't sit right with me at the time. And now I know why. It was you. *You* were the thing he said wasn't important. How does that make you feel?"

She glares at me.

"He didn't know it was me," she snaps.

"He did," I argue. "He looked at the screen. He chose not to answer."

Lindsey clenches her jaw so tightly that I see the muscle tick.

"Did he tell you he was going away with me?" I ask her. "He didn't, did he? He chose last minute to take me away, to distract me because we had just lost our dog, and I was sad. He wanted to cheer me up, because he loves me. And he didn't tell you. That's why you were blowing up his phone. You didn't know where he was. You didn't know we were in a private hut on the water, making love three times a day."

She glares at me. "Three times a day is nothing," she says, her voice venomous. "Three times an hour is more our speed."

My stomach tightens a little. *Our speed.* Hers and Ethan's.

"I thought you were a man," I tell her. "The past couple of months. Whenever he went out after work, he said he was meeting a new colleague. A man named Sam."

I'm putting the pieces together one by one. They're coming together raggedly, their edges cutting me.

Lindsey eyes me with a smirk now. "Do I look like a man?"

"No, you look like a whore." I smile back.

"People don't just grow up wanting to steal someone else's husband," I decide. "There must be something wrong with you. Daddy issues?" I raise an eyebrow, and she rolls her eyes.

"No. I love my father."

"But does he love you? Because that's usually the problem."

She doesn't answer.

Her black skirt is so short that I can see her black lace panties. Of course, her legs are spread wide open.

"Did Ethan buy you those?" I ask conversationally, perching on the edge of the bed. I'm polite now.

She stares me in the eye. "Yes."

I shrug. "Maybe if you were more than a cheap fuck to him, he'd have bought you La Perla like mine instead of overpriced mall underwear."

I know it's mean, but I can't help myself. I have to draw a parallel for her.

She's tacky, and I'm not. She wears drugstore perfume and thinks Victoria's Secret is fancy. She probably drives a Kia. I wear custom perfume, Louboutins, and I drive a Jaguar.

I might be a decade older, but I'm fine wine and she's

Boone's Farm. It's something I have to keep reminding myself because her age bothers me.

"Ethan told me he doesn't love you anymore," she tells me, eyeing me up and down.

"No, he didn't," I answer calmly. "He wouldn't do that."

"You thought he wouldn't do *me* either, but you were wrong about that, too."

Fucking whore.

My rage billows again, and this time I can't stop it. I see red, and before I can register my thoughts, I'm in the bathroom, grabbing red lipstick from my makeup cabinet.

I rush back into the bedroom, leap onto the bed, and straddle my husband's mistress.

I rip her shirt away from her body, and she bucks against me, trying with all her might to get me off. But she's restrained, and I've got rage on my side. It makes my arms wiry, my legs like steel. I clamp my legs around her, and scrawl *WHORE* on her chest in bright red.

Her eyes flash dark in the night, and I jump backward, satisfied.

"You can wipe that away, but you know what you are," I tell her. "Feel those letters on your chest, and know I put them there."

"You're fucking crazy."

She laughs now. She seems so ridiculous, bound in the middle of my bed, yet so cocky and self-assured. That has to change. And it will before this is over.

She has to know how small she is. How much of a *nothing* she is to me, and to Ethan.

"I'm lying in piss," she tells me. "Are you happy now?"

I smile. "I'm getting there. Are you ready to tell me every-thing yet?"

"No. I don't owe you anything."

"Well, then. Sleep well." I get up to leave, and she snaps her head up.

"Wait. Can you clean me up at least?"

"I'm not touching you."

"So, I just have to lie here like this?"

"You're good at lying," I point out. "Especially on your back. Good night."

I glance back at her when I'm at the door. Her makeup is smeared, and her hair is mussed. She's far from the perfect woman I'm sure she tries to portray to my husband.

Now we're getting somewhere.

eight

LINDSEY

I've become obsessed with Tessa Taylor.

Ethan and I have only been together for two weeks, but I have to know what it is about her Ethan is attracted to. What is it that made him want to marry her?

This became a competition from the moment I learned he was married, and I have to know my competition in order to win. I want him, and he wants me. I can feel it. I can see it.

I find myself sitting in the Blush headquarters parking lot at five thirty, after I get off work, right before my seven o'clock class. I know she'll be coming out soon. She's been leaving every day around five forty-five.

Tonight is no different.

She comes out, walking confidently in her fancy shoes and getting into her Jaguar that glistens cranberry red. My nondescript Honda makes it easy to blend into the other traffic as I follow Tessa out of the parking lot and to a grocery store.

I trail her down the cereal aisle and pretend to examine the options while she looks at oatmeal.

"Have you ever tried this one?" I ask her, gesturing to a box.

She glances at me, and her eyes are kind. "No, I can't say I have. It looks good, though."

She's wearing a gray pencil skirt with a black bow around the waist, like she's a gift to someone. Her blouse is white and looks like silk. Her roots are showing ever so slightly.

"I love your hair color," I tell her conversationally, putting the cereal in my cart. "Who do you use?"

"Oh, thank you!" she answers with a smile. "Her name is Julie. I have her card in here somewhere. . . ." She digs in her purse for a minute, then with a triumphant crow, she finds it and hands it to me. "She's great. Such a character. You'll love her."

She can't possibly know that . . . even though we have the same taste in men.

I thank her for the card and put it in my purse. I browse for a while longer, then check out in the line next to Tessa. She swipes her card without a care in the world, like she's never had to worry about an overdrawn bank account.

Once I'm in my car, I pull out the card and call the salon. I ask if Julie can fit me in today. And as luck would have it, she had a cancelation, and "Can you be here in twenty minutes?"

Oh yes, I can.

I drive straight to the swanky salon that promptly serves me a mimosa while I wait. I check my bank account on my phone. I have $176. I'd better just get a cut. I'm sure even that will be expensive here.

They call me back, and Tessa was right. I love her stylist. She's full of chatter and conspiracy theories. I like her instantly, and while she's trimming my hair, she asks how I heard about her.

"Tessa Taylor."

She lights up, tells me Tessa is one of her celebrity clients, and asks how I know her.

I smile. "Oh, we have a mutual acquaintance."

I'm fucking her husband.

Julie snips and combs and chatters about Tessa. "She's so down-to-earth," she tells me. "I didn't expect it. I thought she'd be snobby, but she's not."

I refuse to believe it, even though I remember the smile Tessa had given me at the store. It had been genuine. *Fuck her.*

"Surely, she's not a saint," I say, pretending to gossip.

Julie glances at me, wielding the scissors. "Do you know something I don't?"

I shake my head and giggle, like I'm just being casual.

"She loves her kids," Julie says, tugging on a piece of hair. "Lives and breathes for them. Her oldest . . ." her voice trails off. "She's got a lot on her plate."

"I wonder what her husband is like," I ask casually.

Julie shrugs and hums as she checks my hair. She snips another piece.

"I think her husband is the kind of guy who likes to know he's taking care of something," she finally says. "But then, I think all men are like that to some degree. It's in their DNA. They want to save the damsel, to be the warrior. You know. *Men.*"

I smile conspiratorially and agree. *Men.*

She has given me a thought. He likes to be the savior. Tessa is self-sufficient. She doesn't need him. But I do.

She finishes the haircut, shows me myself in the mirror, and gives me a hug. "Thank you for coming in today," she tells me.

I nod and hand her a ten-dollar bill. She has been helpful, without even knowing it.

I look at Tessa's Instagram in the car. I've gotten to the point where I can't go even a couple of hours without checking it. She's updated her story. My pulse pounds.

"Date night!" she posted twenty minutes ago. "Should I wear this with Strawberry Love lipstick, or this with Lolita Red?"

She posted two pictures. One is the outfit I'd seen her wearing at the store, and one is a little black dress. Her followers are weighing in with their opinions. Most are choosing the black dress with the Lolita Red lip.

Like hell.

I text Ethan.

Come over tonight?

I put my phone between my legs and take a photo of my lacy black underwear.

I send it.

He answers a few minutes later, when I'm at a red light.

I'm sorry, babe. I've got to work.

This is the first time he's refusing me because of his wife.

☹ *Can you stop over on your way home?*

His answer is immediate.

I REALLY wish I could. But I can't. Rain check?

I can't nag. That's what a wife would do, but God, I want to. I want to shout and wave my arms to get him to notice me. Instead, I answer sweetly.

Of course! I look forward to it. ☺

I head home and get ready for class, changing into jeans and a soft shirt. I sit through physiology, all the while checking Tessa's Instagram and Twitter for updates.

She had chosen the little black dress and posted a picture of her and Ethan at a table, clinking their champagne glasses. My blood pressure shoots up a notch. It's not possible that he still loves her. Not when he spends so much time with me.

Yet here I sit.

I look around at the sea of students around me, tired and yawning. They're all six to seven years younger than me.

The difference in our nights is startling. Ethan is with his wife dining in a fancy place while I'm here alone, taking notes about bones. It hardly seems fair and just highlights the mistakes I've made in the past. I should be at the point in my life where I'm sitting in a restaurant with a husband.

I scribble a line of notes. *If a femur and a piece of steel of a comparable size are placed under the same amount of pressure, the steel will snap first.* Interesting, but it's not enough for me. Not when the man I want is sitting with his wife right now. I covertly text Ethan.

You done with work yet? I miss you.

He doesn't answer for a long time, and my mind goes to bad places. Is he having sex with Tessa right now? Is he enjoying himself? What is she doing for him that I don't? Am I not that important to him?

It's forty-two minutes before he answers. He usually answers me right away.

I'm always working. ☺

I stare at the words and wonder what I could possibly say that would make him want to see me instead of his wife tonight, or any night. All nights.

nine

TESSA

Outside, the storm rages.

I sit in the living room, clenching a glass of Ethan's whiskey in my hand as I listen to the howling wind. The ocean is loud and angry. It might be as furious as I am. My knee bounces, evidence of my pent-up agitation, and I leap to my feet, deciding to pace instead.

I throw back a gulp of the liquor, flinch, and do it again. I hate this stuff.

My fingers and toes are numb, but not from the whiskey. From shock. I'm still reeling. I'm like the hurricane—out of control. I don't know what I'm doing. I don't want to be arrested, but I also don't know how to get out of this. *What the hell have I done?*

I'm taking another gulp when my phone buzzes in my pocket. Startled, I reach for it. I have a signal—one flickering bar. Enough for a stream of texts to come in.

Please let me explain.

She didn't mean anything to me.

I've only known her for a few weeks.

I felt so alone, so neglected.

It's not an excuse. I'm just trying to explain.

She came on to me. I should've overcome temptation.

I didn't. And it was a mistake.

I'll be on the next flight, or I'll walk. Either way, I'll be home.

Please be there so I can talk to you.

Please give me a chance.

Please don't leave me.

She meant nothing.

You're everything.

God. My heart squeezes like a vise, so tight I think I might be having a heart attack. I rub at my chest and stare at the words, wondering if any of them are true. How can I know anymore?

He lied to me in the worst way. I gave him my heart, and he broke it. If it's only been going on for a few weeks, and if he doesn't love her, then maybe . . .

I stiffen.

I don't know if I can ever believe you again, I answer.

Then I add, *How could you do this to me?*

But that last one doesn't go through. It gets a red exclamation point as I lose my signal yet again.

I check the other texts that have come in from all three kids.

Connor: *Nonnie is letting us make s'mores on the stove!*

Ava: *I was just looking at your HS yearbooks.*

Ava: *YOUR HAIR.*

Colt: *Mom, I hate that you're out there alone.*

My mother: *Tessa, I can't even get the kids to eat asparagus. You truly need to cook better for them.*

My spine stiffens at the criticism, but before I can truly get annoyed, I hear a pounding in the garage and my head snaps up.

Thunk, thunk. It's loud, and echoes through the house.

What the hell? Is someone here?

I race down the hall, hoping against hope that someone doesn't need my help because I have my husband's lover tied up in my bedroom.

Son of a fucking bitch.

What do I do?

As I step inside the garage, the noise intensifies, but relief floods me as I realize that no one is knocking. Something is rhythmically scraping against the door, driven by the wind.

I manually pull the door open, and a downed palm tree crashes into the garage.

Holy shit.

The wind is already bad enough to down a tree. I grab the trunk and heave it back out of the garage so that I can close the door again. The rain stings my skin. It's coming down so hard, I can't even see the road. I brace myself against the wind, and then slip and slide on the concrete floor, trying to close the door. I yank on the cord and the door hits the ground with an echoing clang.

My hair and shirt are soaked.

It's bad. Maybe even cat four bad. I fumble with the shelves at the front of the garage, hunting for the radio we use during storms.

I find it and turn the power knob.

It's staticky, so I tune it and hunt for news on the weather. It doesn't take long.

"Hurricane Fiona has reached the level of a category four storm. There are reports of 150 mile per hour winds, with an average of 140 miles per hour, sustained. Expect heavy damage. Driving is prohibited. Seek immediate shelter. Fiona will reach landfall within the hour. This is a very dangerous storm and will affect our listening area. Stay tuned to WFSW for more news."

I knew it. The announcer is alarmed, and so am I. The last time we had a cat four, a huge part of our roof blew off and we had extensive water damage. I feel even more isolated now, knowing the voice on the radio is stationed miles from here and I'm alone.

Except for Lindsey.

My shoulders drop, and I take the radio with me to the kitchen. I can hear Lindsey thrashing again, her handcuff banging against my headboard. She's scratching it up I'm sure, but that's okay. I'll burn the entire bed.

"Tessa!" she shouts now. "Tessa!"

Her voice is thin, and I follow it until I'm standing in the doorway again.

"What can I do to get out of here?" she asks. "I don't want to be here."

"You can answer my questions," I tell her simply. "I've told you that from the beginning. I just want to know what happened."

I can hardly look at her now. Looking at her makes her real, but I force myself. She *is* real. She's here. And I have to deal with it.

"But this is between you and your husband," she answers, her eye makeup streaking down her face. "You really should ask him."

"And I've told you, I can't. He's stuck in New York. And you're stuck here. We both are. We might as well make the most of it."

"Take my handcuffs off, at least," she urges. "They hurt."

I look at her handcuffed wrist, and I see the dark shadow of a bruise forming there. I feel bad, but I know what she'll do if I release her.

"Do you think I'm crazy?" I ask her.

"This isn't a fair fight," Lindsey says now. "You've got the upper hand."

My head snaps back, and I stare down at her legs splayed out on the bed.

"A fair fight? Do you really want to talk about a fair fight?" I'm so astounded, I almost can't see straight. "Did you think it was a fair fight when you snuck around with my husband? You were in competition with me, and I didn't even know you existed."

She looks away, not knowing what to say.

"Every time you saw my husband, you made sure everything was perfect, that you said the right things, did the right things. All the while, I was going about life as normal. I was on the phone with our son in my yoga pants and running errands without makeup and being too tired for sex. *That* wasn't a fair fight. I fucking hate you."

"It's not my fault you let yourself go." Lindsey sniffs, and I can't believe she still has the gall to be holier-than-thou, that she still doesn't understand what she did, the part she played. "Ethan said you were always wearing yoga pants and T-shirts, that you never dressed up for him, never tried."

My annoyance hits a limit, and I sigh jaggedly.

"First, that's not true. Second, you're missing the entire point. I've hardly let myself go."

I'd come in here to change my wet shirt. I was going to do it in the bathroom, but I suddenly change my mind.

I strip it off right in front of her. I stand boldly in only my jeans, staring down at her.

"What do you see now?" I ask curiously. "Do you see an old woman? Someone who has 'let herself go'?" I glance into the mirror, at my flat abdomen and long legs. "I'm older than you, but I'm beautiful. You are not prettier than me, not sexier than me. You can lie to yourself about that all you want, but that doesn't make it true."

Lindsey shrugs as best she can. "So can you." She looks me up and down. "If *that* were enough for Ethan, I wouldn't be here."

Her eyes betray her, though. She sees that I truly am competition for her.

But I shouldn't have to compete for my own husband.

I go to my closet and pull out a dry shirt, slipping it over my head, trying so hard to use it to mask my pain. I don't know what I want anymore. It feels like everything I've worked for is a lie.

A *ding* echoes in the room, muffled. I turn around and eye Lindsey.

"What was that?"

"My phone."

Her phone.

Why didn't I think of that before?

I lunge for the purse she'd discarded next to my nightstand and seize it like a prize. Lindsey watches as I drop to the floor, dig through the scuffed-up pink Coach, then triumphantly pull out her phone. It's in a gaudy pink case, something a teenager might buy.

She's got one bar of signal.

"You've got a signal," I breathe.

She's also got fourteen unread messages. My heart pounds when I see Ethan's name on three of them.

Son of a bitch.

My wife knows.

She'll probably try to call you.

Don't talk to her.

That's all he says to her. He doesn't ask how she's doing in the storm. He doesn't ask about her at all. He just instructed her not to talk to me. I stare at her phone, and she looks at me expectantly, her lips curved.

"What? Is it Ethan?" she asks innocently.

I ignore her and scroll up in the thread with my husband. Most of the texts are sexual. They're talking dirty to each other. I feel light-headed, like the room is swirling.

He's a stranger to me, I realize. This side of him is a stranger. How did I not see it before?

I scroll past a weird message from Ethan.

How's Logan doing? Is he feeling any better?

"Who's Logan?" I ask aloud, not voicing the second part of my question: *And why does Ethan care about him?*

Lindsey smirks. "He's my son."

The room spins for a second as I take this in. Not only has Ethan stepped out on me, but he's stepped into another family?

The last remaining piece of my heart shatters into a million pieces.

ten

LINDSEY

As I drive to Marnie's, the restaurant I'm meeting Ethan at tonight, the sky clouds over, and I worry it might rain. I don't want him to see me looking like a drowned rat, but I'm in luck; the weather holds.

It's almost like Fate is on my side, and I even manage to snag a parking spot near the door.

Fate loves me.

I text Ethan.

Are you here yet?

I'm close!

I wait in my car until I see his huge, shiny Ford truck pull into the lot. Its powerful engine rumbles, like it's built to work. It fits Ethan.

He parks in the back, and when he walks to the door, I'm waiting for him there.

Once again, he's dressed in expensive jeans and a crisp white button-down. His initials are embroidered on the bottom, near his belt buckle, in white thread. He smiles when he sees me, and it looks like he sucks in his breath.

I smile back. I look like a Siren tonight.

He opens the door for me, and my heart flutters. We're seated in a booth in the back. No one glances twice at us.

"How was your day?" he asks me, completely casually, because even though we have to sneak around right now, we're a couple.

I smile. "It was fine. Better now."

He flushes, and I find that adorable.

I wish I'd sat next to him instead of opposite him, but at least this way he has a clear view of my cleavage. I see him try not to look but fail. He sees me notice and flushes again.

"How was yours?" I ask politely.

"Better now."

I grin. We order drinks, a beer for him, a Long Island for me.

"Can you drive if you drink that?" he asks. It feels good that he's worried for my safety.

I nod. "Yeah. If it's just one."

He stares at me, a smoldering look that ignites my bones.

"I have to tell you something," he says quietly.

I wait.

"I feel really guilty," he says now, and my heart hammers. This won't do. I reach out a hand, laying it on his arm.

"Don't," I say softly. "With your son and that stress and your wife's job, it's an unusual circumstance, and if no one ever finds out, no one will get hurt."

He stares at me again, and a muscle twitches in his jaw. He's thinking about it.

"I like to think I'm an honorable man," he says finally. "This isn't . . . honorable."

"Are you going to treat me with respect?" I ask bluntly. He nods.

"Of course."

"Then it's honorable."

He shakes his head. "I meant I'm breaking a vow to my wife. I've never done that."

I pretend to think on that. "Honestly, Ethan, she's sort of broken a vow to you already. She was supposed to protect your marriage, nurture it. And she's allowed something else to come before you. I understand that her son and her job are important to her, but she needs to learn to balance everything. She can't let her son's issues or her work affect your marriage. That's not fair."

"It doesn't feel fair," he agrees. "It's not easy on her either. She chews Xanax like candy, and her mind is constantly spinning."

"Not your fault," I point out again, but my brain has already assimilated that information, and I'm flattered that he's told me. She's in trouble. And he's here with me.

"But . . ."

"No buts." I smile as sensuously as I can. "Let's just see what happens. This is between us. When we're together, nothing else exists. Not your marriage, not your bills, not your life at home. Just us."

He picks up his menu, but I can tell he's still thinking about it. I smile behind my own as I choose what to eat.

"Listen." I lower my menu. "There's something I need to

tell you, too. I wanted to wait and see where we were going to go, and it wasn't relevant. . . ."

Ethan eyes me over the top of his menu.

"Okay," he says uneasily.

I laugh. "Don't worry. It's nothing bad."

He waits.

"I have a son. Logan. He's eight."

Ethan's eyes widen. "Oh! I had no idea."

"I know. He's actually in Phoenix right now with my mom. I'm trying to save the money to get him here with me."

Ethan puts down his menu and studies me, his forehead wrinkled. "Why did you have to leave him there? Did you have to come to Florida for a reason?"

I sense the judgment I've heard from so many people. I guess, on the surface, it sounds bad.

I sigh. "It's hard to explain. I swear I'm not a bad person, and I try to be a really good mom. It's just . . . I have a very overbearing mother. She made some mistakes in life, and she's obsessed with the idea that I'm going to make all of the same ones."

"Such as?"

"Oh, just things like getting pregnant young. Which I did." Ethan looks at his menu and then back at me.

"A lot of people get pregnant young. Tessa was nineteen when she had Colt."

I feel like he's judging me again. He's comparing me to his wife, and not in a positive light. I rush to fix it.

"I know. It's just that she struggled when I was growing up. My dad cheated on her and then left, and she was all alone. And she doesn't want the same things for me."

"So you came to Florida to break away from your mom's worrying?"

"No. I got a full ride here at Kaiser. Which meant that I didn't have to accept her help for tuition, which would come with the constant nagging. She makes me feel like a failure if I don't choose the things she wants me to. I had to put some distance between us. And unfortunately, since I'm working and going to school, I don't have a lot of money. Childcare is really expensive. I'll bring him here as soon as I can."

"You must miss him so much." Ethan is sympathetic now, and I exhale. Good. He doesn't think I'm a monster.

"God, SO MUCH. You have no idea."

"I miss Colt, and he's just at college. And he's twenty-one," Ethan answers thoughtfully. "If he were only eight, it would kill me. Is there anything you can do to get him here faster?"

"Well, I'm an executive secretary during the day, which is okay money, but not okay enough to pay for childcare every day. With work and then school, he'd be in childcare so much, and honestly, it's better for him to spend that time with my mom than with a stranger."

"What does your mom do for a living? Is she retired?"

I shake my head. "She's a Realtor, so she makes her own schedule. She's able to do her work when Logan is in school, and then she can be with him at night. Once I'm through with nursing school, I can get a first-shift job and do the same thing."

"Good." Ethan nods. "That'll be good for you both."

"I just want to be able to work for what I get," I tell him. "Not have it handed to me. You must understand that. You've worked for everything you have."

He shrugs, not impressed with himself. "I don't have respect for people who don't."

We order and eat, and when we're done, Ethan looks at me. The quiet longing in his eyes almost does me in. He's desperately seeking something, and I'm not sure exactly what it is. A partner who is there for him? Someone who understands him? Someone who takes the time to try?

The potential is exciting.

"Where do we go from here?" he asks now, hesitant. "I don't want to be a terrible person. But I don't want to give you up."

I smile.

"Walk me to my car?"

That wasn't what he meant, I know, but he's obedient. He helps me out of the booth and guides me across the room with his hand on my lower back, the sign of a true gentleman.

When we stand next to my car, I stare into his eyes.

"You're a good man, Ethan Taylor," I tell him. I kiss him on the mouth. Slowly and sweetly, absorbing him, savoring him.

Each kiss is a stepping stone to the next stage. We're working toward something here.

I run my hands across his chest, feeling the hardness there. Then I feel the hardness elsewhere, pushing into my hips. A thrill pulses through me. I kiss him deeper, tasting the spearmint in his mouth, and his hands are tangled in my hair.

He is rock-hard to my softness, and he's everywhere, everything. I feel dizzy as we go further and further, tipping toward the precipice, rubbing, touching, tasting.

The sensations are blinding.

Our hands are desperate.

His breath is raspy as he touches me, grinds into me. His

hand is between my legs when he finally whispers against my neck.

"We've got to stop. We're in public."

I pull away, and he's dazed. I know he wants me as much as I want him. More than he wants his wife. I can see it. I can smell it. I can feel it. He almost got carried away. It's a heady feeling.

He stares at me.

"I'll talk to you tomorrow," I promise.

Then I get in my car and drive away.

eleven

TESSA

I ignore the pain as I eye my husband's mistress.

"You have a son? Poor kid."

"Shut up," she snaps.

"Who would leave her son in a hurricane to come see her lover?" I ask her pointedly, and I almost convulse at the thought. But my next thought panics me. "Is he alone right now?"

The idea of a little kid, sitting alone in this, scared out of his mind . . .

Lindsey shakes her head. "Of course not. I would never. He's out of the state. With my mother."

I open my mouth, then close it again. My own kids are out of the state with my mother. But mine are there for a vacation. Something tells me things are different for Lindsey.

"Does he live there?" I ask.

"That's none of your business," she answers.

"Okay," I shrug, turning to leave.

"Wait!" she calls out. "Can I call him? I need to tell him I'm okay. He'll be worried in this storm. I'm sure my mom has told him all about it."

"How old is he?"

"Eight."

Unbidden, my heart clenches with an emotion only another mother could understand. Allowing her to call anyone would be stupid. She could tell her son to call the police, or worse.

I turn wordlessly and walk to the kitchen while I think. I hunt for the Ritz crackers, grab a tube, and walk back.

Lindsey watches me, and her eyes look empty now, almost haunted. Is this an act?

"Please," she says quietly. "I'll keep quiet the rest of the time. I'll stop screaming. But I haven't been the best about keeping my promises to him. I promised I'd call today, and I know he'll be worried. Please let me. I won't say a word to him about where I am."

I waver. She sounds sincere, and I'm generally a good judge of character. I'd be a monster if I didn't allow this. I'm a mother, not a monster.

I think for a minute. I'll stand right next to her, waiting to snatch the phone away if I have to. Or better yet, I'll put it on speaker.

"It's under Rita Vale," Lindsey says, as she watches me scroll through her contacts. I find it and press Call, putting it on speaker.

"If you try to say anything to him about being here, I'll end the call," I caution her.

She nods.

On the third ring, a little boy answers.

"Mommy!" he cries, and he sounds so happy. "I thought you weren't going to call."

"I promised I would," Lindsey says, voice taut. "How are you today, honey?"

She pulls her wrist against the restraint, and I see the angry welt forming beneath the metal. There is a bit of blood caked around the cuff. I fight the guilt in my heart.

"I'm good! Gramma took me to the zoo, and we saw them feed the tigers. One kept watching me while it ate, and it freaked me out."

Lindsey smiles, and it actually reaches her eyes. "Well, it couldn't get to you, sweetie. You were safe."

"Are you okay?" he asks abruptly. "Gramma said there is a bad storm there. Will I be there before the next bad storm? I want to see one."

She chuckles a little. "I don't think you really want to see one of these, honey. And I'm planning things."

"That's what you always say," he says, sullen now. "And you haven't come yet."

"That's because I don't have the money," she says, as though she's reminding him, as though this is a well-rehearsed answer. "I want to be with you more than anything in the world. I'll make it happen."

He doesn't sound convinced, and I'm not sure I am either. Lindsey pauses.

"Can I talk to your grandma?"

I promptly end the call.

"You promised," I remind her.

"I wasn't going to tell her anything," Lindsey defends herself. "I just wanted my mother to know where I keep the cash in my house. Just in case."

"Just in case of what?" I lift an eyebrow. Lindsey looks away. "In case you don't make it out of here?"

She doesn't answer.

"If you have a lot of cash stored away, you really should use it to go see your son. You promised."

"Don't tell me how to parent," she spits. "Your life is nothing like you thought it was. You're not really in a position to give me life advice."

"You don't know anything about me," I tell her. She stares back at me, her gaze hard.

"And you don't know anything about me. So shut your mouth."

I stare at her, trying to figure her out. Her kid is with her mom, and she's more concerned with messing around with a married man.

She thought she was meeting my husband here, and she left knowing she was supposed to call her young son. She made the choice to do it anyway and forgo the phone call to assure her son that she's okay in a hurricane. It's unfathomable to me. Who would want to live like that? Juggling a man and her kid, juggling lies?

"Don't you have more respect for yourself?" I ask curiously, and I *am* curious now. "Do you really think so little of yourself? That you believe this is what you are good for?"

She curls her lip but doesn't say anything.

For a moment, just a moment, I see her as a stranger might: a young girl who has made bad decisions and has such poor self-esteem that she thinks she is only worthy of being used. If I were a stranger, I'd feel sorry for her.

But I'm not a stranger.

I open a bottle of water, then I untie her left hand, placing the bottle in it.

"Drink."

She throws it at me, misses, and water splashes across my hardwood floors. I grit my teeth as I get a towel to clean it up.

I return to the kitchen for another bottle. I open it and shove it in her mouth, forcing her to drink.

"You're not going to dehydrate yourself," I say as I dodge her free hand grasping for me. She sputters, and water pours onto her chest like a fountain. "It would be so much easier if you would just act human," I tell her.

She glares at me again, pressing her lips together.

"Fine." I step back. "I don't care if you're miserable."

Hatred burns in her dark eyes, and I feel the fire from here.

"Thank you for letting me call Logan," she says stiffly, unexpectedly.

"You're welcome," I answer, surprised. "Your son shouldn't have to pay for your mistakes."

I hand her the tube of Ritz crackers. She doesn't throw them.

"No, he shouldn't," she agrees. "Also, I misspoke. He's nine. Not eight."

Her voice trembles, almost like she's ashamed she got it wrong.

"I get mine wrong all the time," I say—I don't know why. "Sometimes I even forget how old I am."

"It must be easy to do when there are so many years to remember," she answers. The bitch is back.

I smile ruefully. "Enjoy your crackers."

twelve

LINDSEY

I'm doing laundry when Ethan texts me.

Dinner was nice yesterday!

I smile.
It was. I love getting to know you better, I answer.

I do, too.

I smile again, and he sends another text.

I don't know if this is presumptuous or not.

I wait.

But . . . I have to go out of town tonight. Overnight.
I have a couple of hours of business in Pensacola in

*the morning, then I'll be coming back home. I was
wondering . . .*

I wait.
He doesn't continue. I'm impatient.

You were wondering what?

*I feel silly now. I'm not sure how this is supposed to
work. LOL.*

Well, what were you going to ask?

I was wondering if you wanted to go with me.

I'm stunned. This was fast. I'm happy, though. Very happy.
I have work tomorrow, but I can always call in sick. I haven't
taken a sick day yet, so I wouldn't get in trouble.

While I'm working that out in my head, Ethan texts again.

I was out of line, wasn't I? I'm sorry.

No, not at all! I answer. *I'd love to. I'll call in sick tomorrow. A
little road trip sounds fun.*
Whew, he replies. *I was feeling like a heel.*
Don't, I answer. *I love it.*
I can get you your own hotel room, if you want, he adds.
I roll my eyes.

Don't be silly. That won't be necessary.

We both know what that means. Tonight is the night. My stomach flutters.

We decide that he'll pick me up at six, and I rush about preparing.

I hop in the shower and shave everything completely bare and then shave again. I don't want a single stray hair. I moisturize and blow out my hair, and when I'm finished, I'm perfectly made-up and smell like ripe strawberries—good enough to eat.

I pack an overnight bag, and I'm ready and waiting by six.

It is dusk, so I see the headlights swing into my apartment parking lot. Then he knocks on the door. I invite him in, and his gaze rakes my tiny living space. He sees my bag and picks it up.

"Are you ready?" He's nervous. It's cute.

"I am."

I follow him to the truck, and he opens the passenger-side door for me, helping me in. The leather is cool against my bare thighs.

He gets in and starts the engine, and his fingers are tapping his leg as he pulls onto the road. While we wait at the light, I turn to him.

"Don't be nervous," I tell him. "It's okay."

"I've just never . . ."

He's never had sex with someone other than his wife.

"I know," I tell him. "You're safe with me. I promise."

He seems to relax a tiny bit, though once we hit the highway, his fingers begin tapping again against his thigh, faster with nervous energy.

I wait for a while, and then I grab his hand.

He allows it.

I pull it onto my lap, holding it with both of my own. He's got capable hands. Strong and lean.

"I just thought you deserved something nice," he tells me finally. "You work hard, and I doubt you ever do anything nice for yourself."

I think guiltily about the purse I'd just bought. But other than that . . .

"I can't really afford it," I tell him. "You're very thoughtful."

He smiles at me, so gentle and so satisfied that he's doing something for me. He's so sweet. In this moment, I know that I'll do anything to have him for myself. It's so simple—this touching of hands—but I know with every fiber of my being he wants me.

We ride quietly for over an hour, my head leaned back, my eyes closed, holding a married man's hand.

When we stop for gas, I wait in the truck and fidget.

As he pumps the gas, I notice a hairbrush with hairbands wrapped around the handle in the side of the door. I wonder if it's Ava's or Tessa's. Another jolting reminder he has a family.

I move it to the side and peer beneath it. Napkins, a pack of gum, and two or three crumpled receipts. I twist to look in the back seat of the extended cab.

A sweater, waiting to be worn or forgotten about entirely, is on the seat. It's hard to say which. Other than that, the truck is spotless.

When Ethan climbs back in, he sees the hairbrush in my hand.

"It's my daughter's," he says. "I don't wear pink hairbands much these days."

I laugh and put it back. I like his sense of humor, and I like when he laughs. The corners of his eyes crinkle, truly feeling the laughter.

On the road, I ask him about his kids. He glows with pride when he talks about Connor's kindness and outgoing spirit. "That kid makes me laugh every day," he tells me. "He's just naturally funny."

"What about your daughter?" I ask curiously.

"Oh, Ava. She's so smart. A genius, actually. She's funny, too. And has a really soft heart."

"I think most girls do," I agree.

"She wants to go Ivy League," he adds. "She's very driven."

"That's amazing."

"Having a family is really fulfilling," he says now, gazing sideways at me. "How are you not married yet?"

"Well, I'm only *twenty-six*," I say defensively but purposefully, with a giggle. "I've never felt the need to rush into marriage."

Then I add, "My ex was an ass. I never wanted to marry him. He couldn't keep his dick in his pants, and I was tired of worrying about it."

Ethan clams up immediately, and I realize I've unwittingly drawn another parallel. Between my cheating ex and him.

Damn it.

"Okay, let's not talk about real-life stuff tonight," I suggest.

"What do you want to talk about?" He smiles.

"How about . . . we stop talking?"

I grasp his hand, then guide it between my legs.

Ethan sucks in a big breath as he feels me, his left hand gripping the steering wheel hard.

"Play with me."

So he does.

When we finally reach the hotel, my legs are weak, and my face is flushed. Ethan smiles at me, slow and impish.

"I'll be right back."

I nod and wait, and before long, he's back. He grabs both of our bags, and we head to the room. As soon as we're inside, he drops the bags on the floor and pulls me to him. He kisses me, hard and purposefully, my face in his hands, and then we fall onto the bed. Lightning flashes on the wall as he slides quickly into me, groaning as though he's been waiting for me forever.

We're desperate, panting, and it's over almost as quickly as it began. I'm left dazed, but he reaches for me, again and again. Rain splatters against the window, and we make love for half of the night. With anyone else, it would feel like fucking, but Ethan makes it slow and tender, like I'm fragile. Like I'm important. Like I'm valuable.

When the light hits his face and he reaches for me once again in the morning, he looks at me so sweetly, so gently. I suddenly realize that this simple gaze is all it takes. I'm falling for him. I don't want to ever be without him.

I fall asleep with his arm wrapped around me, thinking of how I can be perfect for him, how I can make him fall in love with me, too.

thirteen

TESSA

I pace in the hall for a while. I don't know what else to do. Nothing is going as I thought, though I never had a plan. All I want is answers, and I'm not getting them.

I check my phone. I still don't have a signal.

How do you make someone tell you things she doesn't want to tell?

I pace some more, and then a thought begins to form.

I go back in the room and pick up Lindsey's phone from the dresser. I look at the texts. Ethan hasn't texted her again, and she still has one bar of signal.

"Ethan texted you," I tell her. "He didn't ask how you are or if you're safe. He simply told you that I know and not to tell me anything."

Lindsey clenches her jaw, and I turn the phone so she can see for herself.

"You'd think he'd at least ask if you're safe," I muse. Lindsey looks away. "Here. Let's try this."

I answer Ethan's text.

She hasn't called me. Are you okay?

"What are you doing?" Lindsey asks, startled. "Don't text him."

"Don't text *my* husband?" I ask, raising an eyebrow.

"Don't text him from my phone," she almost begs. "Use your own."

"I can't. I don't have a signal. You do. Remind me to switch to your carrier after the storm."

Ethan answers the text now, and it distracts me. The sight of his name sends a pang of panic in my heart.

He's betrayed me. He thinks he's talking to Lindsey.

Okay. Good.

I'm on my way home.

As soon as I can get a flight.

"He thinks he's talking to you," I tell her, reading his words. "He's on his way home, he says. As soon as he can get a flight."

My eyes narrow as I realize I can text as Lindsey and get some answers.

What does Tessa know? I text.

Three bubbles pop up. He answers.

*I don't know. I usually delete everything off my iPad,
but I guess I forgot this time.*

Then he sends another.

God, I feel terrible.

I didn't mean to hurt anyone.

I can't help my response. *Well, you did.*
He answers immediately. *I didn't mean to hurt you, Linds.*
Her?
He didn't mean to hurt *her?*
I'm forming a scathing comeback when her phone loses signal yet again. I want to throw it against the wall.

I grit my teeth instead, turning to Lindsey. *She* doesn't know it lost signal.

I smile.

"If you answer my questions, I won't have to text him from your phone," I tell her sweetly, sitting on the edge of the bed, down where she can't kick me.

She eyes me uncertainly. She won't say anything he wouldn't want her to. She's still holding out hope he'll choose her over me.

Will he?

I fight the rush of pure panic that rises in my throat. It doesn't matter who he chooses. It matters what I choose. He's a cheating scumbag. I won't stay with him.

I pretend to tap at her keys, saying my imaginary text out loud. "I think it's best we not see each other anymore," I say. "I don't want anyone else to get hurt."

"Don't send that," she blurts. "Please. I'll tell you everything."

I pause, my thumb hovering over the phone.

"I'm waiting."

"We met online," she whispers. "On a dating website."

Ethan's text from earlier flashes through my head.

She came on to me. I should've overcome temptation.

"On a dating website?" I'm dubious. But she nods.

"Yes."

"Who approached who?" I decide to allow her to continue with her version of the story.

"He did," she says immediately. "He told me my profile was fascinating, and he messaged me his number."

"He sent you his number before you'd even talked to him?"

"Yes."

"You're telling me . . . my husband was on a dating website, that he sifted through the profiles, found yours, was fascinated, and sent you his phone number, sight unseen?"

"We had a connection," she says limply. "I can't explain it better than that."

"I bet." I roll my eyes.

"We did," she insists. "It started with the very first message. He's so funny and smart."

God, that's what attracted me to him in the beginning, too. I swallow hard, trying to dislodge the lump in my throat.

"Tell me . . . how did it progress from a connection and a phone number to sleeping with my husband?"

She looks away, and her foot nervously taps on the bed.

"It was . . . unexpected," she says carefully. "For both of us. He didn't plan to fall for me, Tessa."

"He didn't fall for you," I answer stiffly. "You were just a thing to him."

She swallows hard. "He was kind to me."

"And few are? How hard to believe. I mean, with you try-ing to steal everyone's husbands, and all."

"I'm not a home-wrecker," she sighs. "It just happened. I didn't plan it."

"How long has it been going on?" I ask.

"Almost a year."

That snaps my head back. "That's not possible. Ethan said only a few weeks."

I didn't mean to tell her what Ethan said. But she looks confused, then indignant.

"No. We've been seeing each other since last October."

Nine months. No. No way.

"And for nine months, it just happened?" I ask, my voice shrill now. I clear my throat. "Nine months doesn't just happen. Nine months has a *plan.*"

She shrugs, and I know she doesn't want to betray Ethan.

"When did you sleep together for the first time? Was it right away?"

She shakes her head now. "No. He was sweet. He was really nervous about actually breaking his wedding vows."

Oh God. That makes me nauseous.

"Not nervous enough not to do it, I guess."

"He had a trip for work. He asked me to go with him."

"Where to?" I manage to ask.

"Pensacola."

I think. To my knowledge, he's gone to Pensacola for a job once, an estimate. And it was months ago. Oh God. Is she telling the truth?

If so, I'd spent that night making homemade banana nut

bread, Ethan's favorite. I'd had ten thousand other things to do, but I was trying to do something nice for him. And all while he was out fucking this woman.

"He fell in love with me," Lindsey insists now. "He made love to me that night. We didn't rush into that."

I should've overcome temptation.

Bile rises in my throat, and I can't swallow it. I want to vomit, I want to rail, I want to kill this woman, but instead, I sit as still as a statue.

If she's telling the truth, Ethan is lying. How do I know what to believe? How will I ever believe him again?

I don't know what really happened and what didn't, and that is what kills me. Was he lying when he said she meant nothing? It seems hardly feasible he would risk everything we have for someone who wasn't important to him.

My heart pounds, and I feel panic setting in. I run to the kitchen, digging through my bag to take a Xanax before I return to Lindsey.

"Did you stay with him that whole night?"

She nods now. "Yes. He had to go see someone about a job estimate, then he came to the hotel and got me. We drove back, and he dropped me off before he went home."

I remember how when he'd come home from that trip, he hadn't been interested at all in the banana nut bread. It had stood out in my mind at the time. It wasn't like him. Instead, he'd said he was tired, that he hadn't slept well, that he just wanted to shower and take a quick nap before he needed to go check on a local job site. That's what he had done. He'd immediately showered. When I'd leaned in to kiss him, to welcome him home, he was distant. If she's telling the truth, then it's because he didn't want me to smell her on him. He probably felt guilty or he just didn't want to get caught.

I taste the fury in my mouth. My frustration turns to rage in a cloud of red in my eyes, and with all my strength, I grab a vase and throw it at the wall above the headboard. It ruptures into jagged pieces, and the water rains down on Lindsey. I'm trying to calm myself when I see a blur of movement, coming from the crack between the mattress and the wood, something dark crawling over the shards of porcelain littering the bed.

A spider.

A big wolf spider.

It scuttles toward Lindsey's head and then pauses when it realizes she's a living person. She freezes, her eyes stuck on it. "I don't like spiders," she tells me slowly, quietly. "Please kill it."

Its pincers suddenly move, out then in, and Lindsey screams. The sound startles the spider into motion, and he finds refuge in Lindsey's tangled hair. He burrows in against her neck, and she screams.

I watch as she squirms and cries and begs, and I wonder if she squirmed like that beneath my husband. I can't stop the images that flit before my eyes . . . my husband pleasuring her, Lindsey doing everything he wanted. I squeeze my eyes closed.

"Do something," she cries. "Please."

"No."

I walk away, leaving them together.

fourteen

LINDSEY

"I told you not to call Logan erratically," my mom tells me sternly. "You know as well as I do that you're not going to come get him anytime soon. Please stop making promises and breaking them."

I hear my son playing in the background, making engine noises, and I imagine him on his hands and knees, pushing his little Matchbox cars around. It's a happy thought, and I won't allow my mother to dampen it.

"Mom, things are different this time. I met someone." I can't keep the joy in any longer. I have to share it.

"Oh?"

"He's amazing. Wonderful. So handsome, so successful. He's rich. He's funny. He's an architect. You'll love him."

"He sounds perfect," my mom admits, almost grudgingly. "What's his name?"

"Ethan."

"How old is he?"

"He's forty-three."

"Yikes. That's a bit older than you."

"He's got his life together, Mom. Things are going to be perfect. He's going to be great with Logan. He's got kids of his own, so he knows what to do."

"He's got kids? How long has he been divorced? Do you get along with the ex-wife?"

I swallow. I knew this would come up. I could lie, or I could just be truthful and be done with it.

"He's got three kids," I answer. "They seem delightful, although I haven't met them yet. The timing isn't right. He's not divorced. Yet."

"Oh, Lindsey Elizabeth," my mom sighs, drawing my name out. "I should've known. How could you be so stupid?"

"I know how it sounds," I rush to say. "But it's not like that. I think I love him, Mom."

My mother is quiet, assessing me, judging me.

"You know what your father did to me," she finally says. "You know that he left me for some hussy. And I can't believe that after all the pain we went through when you were little, you'd be the hussy to someone else."

"Mom," I say firmly. "It's not like that. His marriage was already failing. His wife is so wrapped up in herself that she doesn't even notice him anymore."

"And you know that for a fact?" Mom asks me. "Or is that what he tells you?"

I'm silent.

"Has he told his wife he's leaving?"

I remain silent.

"Let me tell you something, Lindsey. I've been around

awhile. And while your father actually left us for another woman, most do not. He's going to use you for everything you've got, and then he's going to leave you. He's got a family with that woman. He's not going to leave her for you."

"You're wrong," I blurt. "He will."

"Has he told you that?"

"Not yet. We're taking our time."

I hate her judgment. I hate that she doesn't know my situation, yet she thinks she does. She hasn't seen how Ethan looks at me. She hasn't heard his voice, so husky and soft, when he's whispering into my ear. The mere thought turns my insides to jelly.

"You just don't understand," I tell her. "Listen, I'm just mentioning it to you because I want you to know my circumstances are going to change. And I'll actually be able to come get Logan. He'll live here with us, and then you won't have to worry about him, or me, anymore."

"Oh, Lindsey." She's so disappointed now. I've heard this tone in her voice a thousand times before. "Please rethink this. You don't need to break up a marriage to be happy. You can build your own life. Come home. I'll help you get on your feet, and you can be with Logan."

"Mom, I love him," I interrupt. "I can't come home. This *is* home."

"You're going to be disappointed," she finally answers. "And Logan, too. He deserves better than this."

And then my mother hangs up on me.

I sit, awash with her disapproval and her warnings. Would Ethan really not leave Tessa for me?

His conscience is so strong. He's always feeling guilty for

betraying her. Eventually, he'll see that he wants me, that he's tired of the guilt, and he'll make a choice. And it will be me. I know him. I'm getting to know him better every day.

But she's known him longer, a voice whispers in my mind. *She knows him better.*

No, she doesn't, I insist to myself. I know the Ethan he is now, and his wife doesn't bother to try.

I get off the couch and dig out some clothes. It's the weekend, and I wish Ethan were here. I text him.

Hey, wanna hang out today? ☺

He answers immediately. *I wish. Colt and I are car shopping. Save me.*

I send him back a crying-laughing emoji.

Maybe tonight? I add.

Maybe! I'll keep u posted.

I chew my lip and set my phone down. Obviously he has to do stuff like this. He'd mentioned last week that Colt needed a new car, and being the good dad he is, he's getting him one. I love that about him. He even asks about Logan. That makes my heart smile, and I get dressed, pull my hair up in a pony, and slap a ball cap on.

Saturdays are perfect. You can do anything you want to do. And what I want to do is find out more about Ethan's life. It's a pull that I can't ignore. I don't want to pry and ask him, but I have to know more.

I get into my car and drive to his address. I can't help but admire how remote his property is. How quiet. The only noise is the sound of the birds chirping. There are only a couple of homes nearby, so rare for a beachfront.

I think for a second and park down the street. I walk back up the road and disappear into the trees, making my way close enough to see the house.

It's got so many windows. That's the first thing I notice. As I get closer, I can see inside. I hug the tree line and make sure I'm tucked out of sight. They must've paid a mint for this.

I slip around the side and down the wooden steps to the beach behind the house, the perfect vantage point. The back of the house abuts a wide veranda, filled with nice patio furniture and a built-in outdoor kitchen. The entire back side of the house is encased in windows, giving them beautiful views of the ocean and making my job easy.

I see Tessa trudging into the kitchen in her bathrobe, her hair pulled back into a sloppy ponytail as she pours herself a cup of coffee. She sits at the kitchen table and drinks it. She doesn't move from there for a long time. I see her scanning through her phone, using one finger the way middle-aged people do. She looks tired, and at eight in the morning in her own kitchen with no makeup, she is a bit different from the glamorous photo on her website.

I have the advantage of knowing that I need to be perfect. Whenever he comes over, I make sure that I'm perfectly made up, that my breath is always fresh, that my snatch is always shaved. It's exhausting, and some days, it feels damn near impossible. I mean, no one is perfect.

But I have to be. I'll continue losing sleep and burning the candle at both ends to make it so.

I have to show him that I'm better . . . that I'm the right one for him.

I never want him to see me looking like Tessa does right now.

Ava walks into the kitchen, teenaged and sleepy. I'm surprised to see her up this early. Kids usually aren't. She rubs at her eyes and opens the big fridge. I see the logo on the door. Viking. Of course.

She pulls out orange juice, pours a glass, and sits next to her mom, her head on her mother's shoulder. Tessa types on her phone, then sets it down, and pats her daughter's back.

Is something wrong?

But Ava pulls her head back, and they laugh together, immersed in a joke I can't hear. Tessa loops an arm around Ava's shoulders, and I find myself envious for a second. I never had that with my mom. Granted, my mom worked all the time. She had to work two, sometimes three jobs just to support me. Which is why I work so hard now. So I won't have to later, and Logan will have a good life.

But this. I look at the house, at Ava and Tessa inside. This is beyond good. This is perfect.

"Hey!"

A voice startles me out of my thoughts, and I see a teenage boy jogging down the wooden steps toward me, a yellow surfboard held easily under his arm.

"Can I help you? This is a private beach."

I realize how this looks, standing at the base of the stairs, staring into his house.

And it is his. I'm looking at Connor Taylor. I recognize him from the pictures.

"I'm sorry." I smile. "I came out for a morning walk. I'm staying with one of your neighbors, and I guess I got turned around. All the houses look the same from the back."

I laugh, and he smiles at me.

"They do," he agrees. "There are only three here, though. Who are you staying with? Millie and Ed, or Bob and Susan?"

"Bob and Susan," I say immediately. "Just for the weekend."

Connor reaches the bottom step now. "Oh, cool. My mom wanted to take them some jelly she bought in New York. I'll let her know they're home. We thought they'd gone to Michigan."

Damn it.

It doesn't matter, though. I'll be long gone when they find out.

"Your beach is beautiful," I tell him. "You surf?"

"Before I could walk." He grins, an easy smile, broad and open and trusting. His eyes are Ethan's, and the similarity punches me in the gut. This is Ethan's son. I'm standing here talking to Ethan's son.

He winks at me and then jogs directly out into the water, without pause. He paddles out to the break and waits there.

I wonder if they have any idea how fortunate they are. Very few people get to live like this. Palm trees sway and dance up on the bluffs, the ocean crashes soothingly. Their house is practically a palace.

It's not fair. I fight the green jealousy that claws its way up from my belly.

I'm trying to do everything right so Ethan will want a relationship with me, and they're here, doing nothing to earn it. They just take it for granted. I bet none of them have worried a day in their lives.

I think of Colt, the oldest, and I know they have worried. About him. But not about their lifestyle. Not like me. They don't know what it's like to fight to survive, to want nice things and a better life.

In front of me, Connor crouches on the board, his red trunks bright in the sun. The wave carries him easily, and he effortlessly stands and rides it. He's been doing this for a long time, I can see. He's had luxuries I've never even known.

He's grinning when he reaches the shore, and from here, backlit from the sun, he is the spitting image of his dad. I'm sure Ethan looked exactly this way when he was Connor's age. Young, strong, full of energy and confidence. It reminds me of how handsome Ethan is. How seasoned and refined.

As Connor paddles back out, I pull out my phone.

Missing you! I text him. *I really want to see you tonight.*

I want to see you, too! He answers. *I'll make it happen!*

Satisfaction buoys me, and I watch Connor for a few more minutes, until I decide it's creepy if I continue. I'm just starting to climb the stairs when someone appears at the top of them. Immediately, I tug my ball cap down.

A female voice calls to Connor.

"Come on, sweetie! You've gotta shower."

I glance up, and Tessa looks far different now, in just the space of twenty minutes. She's dressed, put together, and ready for the day.

I put my head down and walk away, confident that I am, too.

I'll be seeing her husband tonight.

fifteen

TESSA

I stand in the garage, trying to see out through the rain. The storm shows no sign whatsoever that it is letting up anytime soon.

I try to still my pounding heart as I pull down the door again and secure it.

As I walk back into the main house, I bump one of Ava's paintings hanging along the hallway. I pause and straighten it. Just like her, it is bright, colorful, and beautiful, an abstract of reds and pinks and turquoises in the shape of a heart on a smeared blue background. I smile just thinking about her bubbly personality, her quirky sense of humor, and then Lindsey screams for me.

I stalk to the bedroom. I pick up her phone and check the texts. Nothing new has come in. I search for a thread from her mother. There is one, but nothing is new there either.

Lindsey whimpers, and the tiny pieces of the shattered vase

have made her bleed in various places, her legs, her arms. I feel a flash of guilt.

"What?" I demand.

"Can you just check for the spider?" she asks, her voice empty. "Please?"

It's hot now. With the power off, the A/C hasn't been running for hours, and the bedroom is stifling. Sweat pours off the girl on my bed, and I bend over her, examining her hair.

"Oh yes," I murmur, as I poke through it. "There it is."

She starts to shriek again, but I put my hand on her arm.

"Stop. It's dead."

There are bits of it in her hair, and she rolls wild eyes at me.

"Please, can you get it out? I'm begging you."

Her legs are splayed and sweaty, and she smells like body odor and piss. She looks pathetic. I think of Ava and how she's terrified of sea gulls. What if Ava were in this position and someone was leaving her with the corpse of a dead bird?

With a sigh of resignation, I grab my comb and reluctantly comb through Lindsey's hair to get the spider out.

"Thank you," she whimpers. "Thank you."

I ignore the relief in her voice, and I pull the remnants of the carcass from her hair.

"You don't look as old as I thought you would," she says now. Is this her version of a compliment?

"I'm only forty," I remind her. I take the comb to the bathroom and rinse it off. I glance in the mirror. I don't look a day over thirty-five. Maybe even thirty-two. I've been very careful with my skin ever since we moved to Florida.

"I can see why Ethan used to love you," she says as I return to the bedroom. My heart flinches at the phrase *used to*. I try to keep my face impassive. "You've got class. Except for the kidnapping, of course."

"It's not kidnapping if you came here of your own volition," I tell her.

She rolls her raccoon eyes.

"Whatever. I'm trying to give you a compliment."

"Why? Why bother? You are not my friend. You are trying to steal my husband."

"Because you let me call my kid. Because you got the spider out of my hair. You aren't a terrible person, or Ethan would never have loved you in the first place."

"Listen, don't patronize me," I snap. "He doesn't love you. If he told you he does, he's lying. I'm his wife. You're not. He told me you're nothing to him."

She flinches, and I should feel sorry, but I don't.

"You don't believe that he contacted me first, do you?" she asks, studying me. "You think I'm lying about everything."

"I don't know what to think. But that definitely doesn't sound like Ethan."

Ethan is shy with women. He'd never put himself on a dating site.

"Okay. Look at my phone," she suddenly says. "There's an app on there. All the Fish. Pull it up."

Why didn't I think of that earlier? Honestly, my brain is still in a fog, still in shock. I haven't been thinking right.

I pick up her phone, find the app, then open it. I see her profile there on her homepage, then I click into her messages. They're all from one person. My husband.

123

My mouth goes dry as I scroll through them, and then I get to the first one.

> Hey. You're so beautiful, and your profile is
> fascinating. Here's my phone number. Check out
> my profile and see if you're interested. ☺

My husband was on a dating site.

He was actively searching for someone new. I look at the date. It was, in fact, last October. Lindsey was telling the truth. This has been going on for a long time, and he definitely contacted her first. The proof is in front of me.

I should've overcome temptation.

The room spins, and I click on his name and look at his profile. His profile picture is from the beach. I distinctly remember the photo, because I'd been in it, too. He'd cropped me out. The bastard is using a picture of the two of us, with me cropped out, to lure other women to him.

My stomach hits the ground, and I try to hide my discomposure from Lindsey. She's watching though, and she knows. She blinks.

"See? I'm sorry."

"No, you're not." I hate her all over again.

She blinks. "Listen, I never considered you in this. It was about me, and him."

"It was never just about you and him," I snap to her. "Not when you were pursuing a married man. When did he tell you?"

"On our first date."

"And you stayed around after that? Classy."

"He said he wasn't happy," she insists. "That you never made time for him."

"He never said a word of this to me!" I don't know why I'm telling her this. "If that's true, he would have at least tried to talk to me about it. None of this makes sense."

"My dad cheated on my mom, and it destroyed her life. I personally have an ex-boyfriend who used to cheat. I would never purposely wreck someone's home. It just happened."

"Nothing ever *just* happens," I answer, and my words are as ragged as my heart. "Especially something that 'just happens' for nine months. That's long enough to carry a child."

"It's different with Ethan and me," she insists. "I swear. In fact, he stuck with me through a pregnancy scare. If he didn't love me, he would've been gone."

A pregnancy scare.

I lift an eyebrow. "Ethan had a vasectomy. If you got pregnant, it wasn't his."

I think back around the fog in my head. When did he have that surgery? Was it two years ago? That would've been before he met her. But wait, it was right before Connor went to the state championships. Ethan was too sore to go, and that was just . . . less than a year ago.

Fuck.

"When was your scare?" I ask her bluntly, not mincing words.

She thinks on that. "Last November."

Son of a bitch. Ethan had his vasectomy in November.

If she's telling the truth, maybe there was a pregnancy scare, and Ethan chose not to end it with her, but instead he immediately ran out and got a painful surgery to prevent any future scares. I tell her as much.

"You're lying. Ethan wouldn't get a vasectomy after meeting me," Lindsey tells me, confident now. "We're going to have a family. We've talked about it."

"Ethan already has a family!" I scream, my blood boiling and my vision blurring. "And he most certainly did get a vasectomy. We don't want any more children. We're done. He sat in our living room for an entire weekend with a bag of frozen peas on his balls."

I had laughed at the time. *Ethan, I had my tubes tied after Ava. There's no way we're going to get pregnant.*

Let's just be sure, babe, he'd said. *We don't want a surprise this late in life.*

He'd cited the small percentage of failed tubals and miracle babies, and it had made sense at the time. I'd just shrugged and agreed. If he wanted to go through extra pain for some extra assurance, that was his business.

I hadn't questioned it. *Why hadn't I?*

"You're wrong," she says simply.

And then I lose it. My vision is red as I thrash about the room. I glance at a large wooden picture with words from the Song of Solomon on it. *I am my beloved's, my beloved is mine.* I rip it down and smash it into the wall. My shoulders ache, but I don't care. I need to break things. I need to destroy something the way I've been destroyed.

"You don't see how he didn't really want you?" I shriek. "He lied to you, you idiot. Just like he was lying to me."

Lindsey stares at me now, and I can see her thoughts in her eyes. *Am I telling the truth? Did Ethan really prevent future children with her?* She shakes her head, not wanting to believe, and that just enrages me further.

"You dumb bitch! You really think that he'd have some sort

of an allegiance to you?" Bile rises in my throat as I rage. "You're delusional."

But the idea, the fact, that Ethan altered his body so he could continue playing with this girl guts me. It infuriates me. And she simply refuses to see that he was doing just that: playing.

"He was playing house with you!" I try to take deep breaths and rein myself in. "He didn't want anything real with you. He didn't want substance. He wanted sex. He wanted his ego stroked."

"He wouldn't do that," Lindsey calls from behind me as I walk out of the room.

Yeah. That's what I'd thought, too. But he had.

I have her phone with me, so I curl up in the living room with it and Ethan's bottle of whiskey. The heat is unbearable. I wipe the sweat from my eyes, and it smears on Lindsey's phone screen.

I dig further into her dating app and study my husband's dating profile. He lists his name as Nicholas. That's his middle name, so it's not exactly a lie. He likes sailing, sunsets at the beach, and James Bond movies. All true. He's six-four, light brown hair, hazel eyes. All true.

He's single. False.

The lie leaps off the screen at me, and I swig at the liquor.

Fuck him. Fuck. Him.

The liquid burns my throat as I swallow and log out of the app. I try to log back in with Ethan's email and the password he always uses. No luck.

I want to see his messages. I want to see who else he attempted to contact.

Did any of them get back to him? Why did he choose Lindsey?

As handsome as my husband is, I'm sure he had his choice. So why her? How did he let the others down?

Why do I care?

I hate whiskey, but I take another drink, then another. I feel light-headed, a bit dizzy. I'm not sure how much of it is this horrible situation and how much is the liquor.

I take the bottle, march back to my bedroom, and lean against the doorjamb. Lindsey is a sweaty mess, covered in urine, her eye makeup streaming down her face, but even still . . . she's young and beautiful. She looks vulnerable now, lovely in a tragic way.

Fury lights me up all over again.

How dare she?

I'm doing my best to break her, to make her see, and it's not working.

"Let's go back to my question to you earlier," I tell her. *Are my words slurring?* No. I'm not that drunk. "Do you have daddy issues because your daddy doesn't love you?"

It's as though my words are an arrow through her heart, and I watch her face crumple as my words pierce her. Her mouth puckers, and her chin wrinkles. Is she going to cry?

I wait, and she doesn't. She pulls herself together. It's impressive.

Her face is a steel mask as I study her.

"The apple doesn't usually fall far from the tree," I spit out. "Your dad taught you it was okay to break vows, to hurt the ones you love. You could've chosen to learn from that, though. Not to emulate it."

"I didn't emulate it," she spits. "I'd never be like him."

"But you are. Don't you see it?" I screech.

She's silent, and I decide to connect the dots for her.

"Your father thought it was okay to destroy someone else's family, just because he wanted the girl for himself. You tried to destroy my family just because you wanted my husband. It's the same thing!"

"You don't understand." Lindsey's voice is soft and thin, a complete contrast to my elevated tone. "You don't understand what it's like to be me."

I snort, hardened now. "Why? Because you haven't been handed things in life? Because you had an absentee father? Wake up! That's life. I've had to work for what's mine, and you should, too. You can't just take things."

"You'd never understand." Lindsey shakes her head. "Nothing I ever do is right. No matter how hard I work, nothing turns out. I'm a disappointment to my mother. I got pregnant when I wasn't married. The father didn't want anything to do with us. She saw me making all of her mistakes, and I failed her. Do you know what that's like?"

She's trying to appear human now. To appeal to my soft side. It doesn't work.

"I don't give a shit!" I screech. After a few moments, I slide to the floor with my back to the wall just inside the room. The bottle and phone still in my hands, I get ahold of myself.

"My relationship with my mom isn't that great either," I finally reply. "She criticizes me constantly. But I never, *ever* thought it would be okay to break my marriage vows. Some people decide to be the opposite of what they hate. You've chosen to be the same."

"I don't hate my father," she tells me. "I never had the chance to love *or* hate him."

"Cry me a river," I spit. "We're all damaged. You are *not* a victim. Yet you've got this chip on your shoulder that makes you think you are, and that because of it, it's okay to hurt people to get what you want."

I take another drink of whiskey. It no longer burns.

"Your dad cheated on your mom. Somewhere, deep down, you've registered that behavior as normal, as a line that is okay to cross. I'm here to tell you, it isn't."

"So you're saying it's my father's fault I'm the way I am?" she asks. I'm already shaking my head.

"Good God. No! I'm saying your behavior is your own. You make your decisions, just like Ethan makes his and I make mine. You need to grow up, handle your issues, and stop using them as crutches to hurt people."

I get up to leave, but pause. "God, it smells in here."

I grab the perfume bottle from my dresser and spray it onto Lindsey.

"That's five-hundred-dollars-an-ounce custom perfume," I tell her. "Next time you want a boyfriend to buy you something classy, try looking outside of the mall kiosks."

I walk out and don't look back.

I fight the feeling that grows inside of me . . . the one that says I went too far, the one that says I should stop. It grows like a black shadow, overtaking my need for revenge. I try to fight it back, to banish it, because I'm not done yet.

But even still, when I sit in the living room and bury my face in my hands, I see Lindsey's face when I mentioned her father.

It was the broken face of an abandoned little girl.

sixteen

LINDSEY

I roll over and automatically reach out for Ethan, but he's gone.

I open an eye, and the sunlight is too bright. Of course he's gone. He left before I fell asleep. I sigh and sit up, rubbing the sleep out of my eyes. I catch a whiff of his cologne, and I grab his pillow, inhaling it. It smells just like him. I smile.

I text him and tell him. He answers back with a smiley face.

Then he follows up with: *Have a great day, beautiful!*

I trudge to the kitchen and make some coffee, then scroll through my phone, trying to decide what to do with my Sunday after I finish homework. But then, sitting here, in the morning sunlight, I realize the absence of something.

Cramps.

I should be on my period right now. I'd marked it on my calendar so that I'd know when to plan dates with Ethan.

I'm not on my period.

My heart suddenly hammers hard in my chest. I'm never

late. A thousand scenarios pop into my head, but the only one I can focus on is . . . I could be pregnant, and Ethan would think I did it on purpose.

I take my pill religiously, every night when I brush my teeth. Because of that, Ethan doesn't use condoms. I'd assured him that I was clean, and he'd taken my word for it. What if the pill had failed?

Oh my God.

What would happen? Would he leave Tessa? Would he hate me? Would he think I did it on purpose? Or worse . . . would he wonder if it was even his?

I pace around and gulp at the coffee, placing my hand on my flat stomach.

I don't want to be pregnant. But what if I am? And Ethan's true intentions are revealed? I feel a little nauseated.

I'm scared to tell him. I'm excited, terrified.

Could I do things over as a mother, do it right?

Oh my God, what will Logan say?

I pace some more.

My phone rings.

"Hey, pretty." It's Ethan. "I'm out running a few errands. Are you home?"

"Yeah," I tell him absently. "I am."

"Good. I'm gonna stop by."

"Didn't you wear yourself out last night?" I ask, smiling, joking, acting like everything is fine. It's fine, it's fine, it's *fine*.

"That was then," he answers. "This is now."

He hangs up. I normally would be fluttering around, trying to get ready, but today, I'm distracted. I'm scared about the possibilities. If I'm pregnant and I get fat, he might not want me anymore. He might not want to go through the ups and downs of pregnancy hormones or morning sickness.

No, that won't happen. Tessa had three babies. He's still with her.

Maybe he'll see it as a miraculous surprise. He wasn't expecting to ever have more kids at his age, I'm sure. It's a gift. *Right?*

Actually, maybe this whole situation is a gift.

I'm still not dressed when Ethan taps on the door a few minutes later. I'm only in a T-shirt and panties, and when I answer, he grabs me and runs his hands up and down my hips.

"You look rode hard and put away wet," he murmurs into my ear. "I wonder . . . who would've done that to you?"

I smile, but my heart is still pounding. This is good.

He can't think it's not his.

I kiss him back, hard, urgently, and he fucks me against the bathroom island. The edge bites into my back, but I don't care. All I care about is the warm fluid that shoots into me when Ethan climaxes.

There it is.

I relax, gripping his hair.

This is a reminder to him that we have unprotected sex and that this baby is his.

Ethan is damp with sweat as he helps me stand straight, and he smiles when I look wobbly. He thinks it's because of the sex.

"I'm late," I blurt out, and Ethan smiles.

"Late for what? I'm sorry. I didn't know you had plans."

"No. I'm *late.*" I gesture toward my belly. Ethan's eyes widen, and his mouth drops open ever so slightly.

"Oh. God." He stares at me, shocked, and I rush to explain.

"I didn't miss a pill. I don't know why this would happen. It wasn't on purpose . . ."

I pause, and Ethan is motionless.

"I'm sorry," I tell him.

"Are you sure?" he asks seriously, and his eyes have gone flat, the afterglow of sex completely gone.

I shake my head. "No. I'm just . . . I'm never late."

"We should get a test."

"Yeah," I agree.

"I'll be right back."

Ethan is out the door without another word. I walk to the window and watch as he rushes to his truck and drives away.

That wasn't really the reaction I wanted. I was looking more for something along the lines of, *No matter what, we'll be okay.* Or *I support you no matter what.*

But instead, he'd rushed away.

I'm showering when he returns, my head buried under the waterfall of water, the steam hiding my tears.

"I've got a pregnancy test," he announces from the doorway. "Can you take it when you're finished?"

There's a knot in my throat when I answer. "Yes. Of course."

I take my time, shaving my legs, conditioning my hair. I don't know that I'm ready to know for sure. My life could completely change right now. We could be at an impasse, a fork in the road. I want to know . . . I don't want to know.

But time waits for no man, and I pee on the stick as Ethan paces outside.

I wait. He waits. Each on opposite sides of the door.

134

When the second line doesn't form, I don't know if I'm disappointed or happy.

"I'm not," I call.

"Thank Jesus," he breathes, and my stomach drops.

I toss the stick into the trash, trying to ignore the resentment brewing in me. *So what if I had been?*

He hugs me when I come out, and he's vastly relieved. I allow it, but I'm not that receptive. He notices.

I curl up on the couch and face him. He comes to sit next to me.

"Aren't you happy?" he asks, confused, his hand on my thigh.

"Yeah," I sigh. "I just . . . it would've been nice to know that you have my back no matter what."

"I do," he protests. "It was negative, so you didn't get a chance to see that. I have your back."

I look at him. "So if it had been positive, what would you have done?"

He's quiet, and his hand is still.

"I would've handled it," he finally says.

"What does that mean?" I ask, unrelenting. "You would've left Tessa? You would've paid for the abortion? What?"

"Don't say that," he says quickly. "I didn't ask you for that."

"Because I wasn't pregnant," I point out slowly. "But what if I had been?"

"It's a moot point," he answers. "Because you aren't. Let's not borrow trouble."

"Look." I face him and take his hand off my leg, holding it in my own instead. "I don't know what we're doing here. I want to have fun and see where things go, but at the same time, we have to have a purpose, you know? Otherwise, what are we even doing?"

He's uncertain and slow to answer, but I stay the course. I stare at him, waiting.

He flushes.

"I don't know," he finally answers, and it's such a letdown from this confident, successful man.

"You want me, right?" I ask him, staring into his eyes.

He nods. "Of course."

"Then I don't understand your hesitation."

"I have an entire life," he says, awkward now. "Outside of you. I have a kid in college, one about to be, and then one more later. Tessa and I . . . our lives are enmeshed. Our finances . . . it would be so complicated."

"But you're not happy with her," I point out. "She doesn't care if you live or die."

"I wouldn't go *that* far," he answers dryly.

"You know what I mean," I insist. "You are my *entire world*. Isn't that important to you?"

"Of course it is." His voice is low, soothing. "You're so beautiful. You're a breath of fresh air in a stale world."

"But do you love me?"

The question comes out before I can stop it and lingers in the air between us. I'm aghast at the words, and I think he is, too. We stare at each other.

"I don't know," he admits. "To be honest, I haven't let my-self go there. I mean, I'm married. It doesn't make sense to get attached. . . ."

"Unless you're willing to change it all for me," I interrupt. "People do it all the time. Their marriages stop working. Things change." I press on. "I want it all. I want to give you everything. I want to give you babies and a happy life. Don't you?"

Ethan opens his mouth, then closes it and pauses. And that pause is so pregnant.

"I don't know what I'm willing to do, Linds," he finally answers. "I think about you all the time. You're so real to me. Tessa isn't. For now, is it enough that I'm risking everything just to be with you?"

His eyes are gold in the light, and he smells so good. It has to be enough. For now. I knew what I was getting into.

"Of course," I answer. "Yes, of course. Today has just . . . been stressful. Let's forget about it."

He pulls me to him and presses a kiss to my forehead. He kisses my neck, then my lips, and I go with it. I have to be his refuge, his escape, his perfection. That's my edge. We make love on the couch.

I cling to him, listening to his heart beat as he slides into me, my hands curling into the couch. I lock my legs around him, pulling him close, closer, into me, which is where he belongs.

He has to want me.

A drop of his sweat drips from his collarbone onto mine, and I want to soak it up, to soak *him* up.

He *has* to want to stay with me.

Want. Me.

I stare into his eyes, and he stares back, and he loves me. I can tell. Even if he can't say it aloud just yet.

I cling to him when we're done, and I only reluctantly let him go. He's thoughtful and quiet when he leaves me.

He hugs me at the door. "I'll call you later," he promises. I nod and watch him drive away.

I spend the rest of the day doing homework . . . chemistry and anatomy. It's bedtime before he texts instead of calls.

A work trip popped up. ☹

I'll be gone for a few days.

I miss you already.

I stare at the words, and I want to ask if I can come, too, but I don't. I can't be too needy, and he's not offering.

It's okay. It's all okay.

It's fine. I'll miss u while ur gone, I answer.

He responds with a kiss emoji.

I'm frustrated. He just needs time. He's on the precipice of his whole world changing, and it's startling. He'll figure it out.

I'm still telling myself that as I fall asleep.

seventeen

TESSA

I sit in Ethan's office, holding the hospital bill beneath the flashlight in my hand.

Line by line, the hospital outlined what was used to make my husband sterile, along with the prices. I flinch when I look at the date, knowing the reason this procedure was necessary . . . was her.

After insurance, we still paid over a thousand dollars for the procedure. A thousand dollars for my husband to safely have sex with someone else.

I wonder how much more money we've spent on Lindsey.

I stiffen my spine.

On his desk, Ethan has a framed photo of the two of us on one side, a family photo on the other. In both pictures, he has his arm wrapped easily around my waist, a familiar touch, a casualness born from years of being together. Years of loving each other. At least so I thought.

But if he loved me, how could he do any of this?

I scan the room. Everything in here has been touched by me. The draperies I chose, the wall color, even the heavy wooden desk. Ethan wouldn't care if he worked on the floor. But I wanted him to have a nice office. Just like I wanted him to have a perfect life. I worked so hard to make it so. And to what end?

Here I sit. And there *she* is . . . just down the hall in our bed.

I stand up and walk to the bookcases lining the far end of the room. Ethan loves to read, and the shelves are filled with his favorites, everything from true crime to the classics.

I trail a finger along the spines as I pace, and it's so hard to take everything in. My mind is a rubber band, expanding and expanding, until it snaps back, unable to fathom everything, unable to understand. Is adultery an inevitability of life? Do men just get tired of their wives and cheat? The thought weighs my heart down. Like jagged rocks on the bottom of the ocean, with each pull of the tide, the rocks rake over my lungs, making it harder and harder to breathe.

My finger comes across something foreign, and I pause, bending to examine it.

A piece of paper is stuck between the neatly shelved books. It's folded, and I wouldn't have noticed it at all if my finger hadn't caught on the pointy edge.

I pull it from the shelf and open it, finding a letter written in Ethan's scrawling handwriting. When I see *Dear Tessa*, my heart drops, and my knees suddenly can't support my weight. I head straight to his desk, sinking into his chair to read.

There is no date on the letter, but the deep crease makes me believe it's been sitting on that shelf for a while. My eyes flit over the words, feeling each one of them in the center of my chest.

Dear Tessa,

I want to start by saying I love you. God, I love you. I love the way you wake up at full-speed every morning, how you always feel there isn't anything you can't do . . . and you're right. There isn't.

I love what a great mother you are. I love what a powerful businesswoman you've become. I love your smile. I just don't see it that often anymore. I feel like we've become strangers, Tess. Two ships passing in the night, bumping our masts in the hall from time to time. Two ships who share children and a bank account and a life.

We share a history; we share stories; we share so many things from the past. But I feel that we've stopped making new stories and new memories. I don't feel like I matter to you anymore, babe. I feel like I'm just another problem for you to solve at the end of the day, one more thing for you to take care of . . . just something else on your to-do list.

I know if I bring this up to you, you'll roll your eyes and you won't understand. You live in the moment, constantly planning for the future, your eyes pointed straight ahead.

I just wish I had some way to make you see me again. I need for you to see me, to want me, to appreciate me.

This sounds so silly as I sit here and write it, while you are at Connor's football game, busy being a great mom. And then, when you come home, you'll still have hours of work to do before you finally come to bed, busy

building your career. And I shouldn't complain. But I just
want a place in your life again.

I miss you, Tess.

I miss us.

I wish I knew what to do.

The letter ends there, without closing remarks or a signature, and I hold the paper in my shaking hands, my exhaling breath moving the page.

When did he write this? How long has he felt this way? Why didn't he give me the letter?

My heart aches at his words, at how obtuse I must've been to not see them on his face. Am I a monster? A terrible wife? What the hell happened to us?

Once upon a time, we were a force to be reckoned with . . . the two of us against the world. And then, somehow, at some point, we started moving in different directions, and neither of us even noticed. Well, *he* did.

I get angry again. If he noticed, he should've said something. Part of being married, of being a team, is communicating. I can't read minds. If he was feeling neglected, it was his job to tell me.

Or should I have just known? I remember my mother's face when she told me to watch all the traveling. Did everyone else know but me?

I think about our sex life, and I realize all at once that Ethan wasn't that into it toward the end. Even the day he left for his trip, it was mechanical, like we were going through the motions.

But isn't that what happens in marriage? Don't people get comfortable?

There's comfortable, and there's neglectful, a voice whispers in my ear. My own conscience. *You know you've neglected him. You thought he'd always be there at the end of the day, the one true thing you could always count on, so you took him for granted. You stopped trying.*

A pang stabs me in the gut.

It's true.

I've been an absentee wife. Focused on everything but Ethan.

My shoulders slump, and I feel completely stupid. Was I born without some sort of intuition on how to keep my husband happy? Am I defective? Is there not a way to be a successful, independent woman in this world while also having a happy marriage?

A beat passes, and then I feel the anger welling inside me again.

He *chose* to cheat on me. He could've talked to me, could've attempted to express his feelings, but he chose the easy way out—ignoring the problem. He could've given me this letter, and I would've *seen* his unhappiness. I would've fixed it. But he didn't. He chose to replace me with a younger version, someone eager to walk in my shoes.

I clench my jaw. Did she really think it would be so great to be me? Did she really think she had that capability . . . *to be me?*

My vision is almost blurred by my outrage. I snatch up the hospital bill and march back to my bedroom. Lindsey's eyes are closed, but they pop open the second the door opens.

"Here is proof of the vasectomy," I tell her, and I put the bill next to her. She looks at it and then at me. I see disappointment in her eyes, though she tries to hide it.

"As you can see, he chose to get fixed so he couldn't *ever* have more children. He never intended to become a father with you, Lindsey."

Fire burns in her eyes now; she's annoyed with me, frustrated with Ethan. But he's not here, and I am.

"You probably pressured him to do it," she says, her lips pinched.

I laugh. "Why would I do that? I had a tubal after Ava. The odds of me getting pregnant are nil. There was one reason, and one reason alone, that Ethan wanted to get sterilized. He didn't want *you* to get pregnant."

Lindsey blinks, her eyelids are camera shutters, closing me out, hiding her thoughts. But I know what she's thinking. She's hurt. She feels betrayed. She feels lied to, used. That she and I are feeling many of the same things right now gives me an odd sense of satisfaction.

"Vasectomies can be reversed," she says, and her words are slow, unconvinced. "He was placating you. He knew he could have it reversed."

I laugh. "You need to listen to me," I instruct sharply. "As God is my witness, I had *nothing* to do with his vasectomy. It was his idea, his decision. I didn't feel it was necessary. He made this decision because of *you*. Not me."

"That's not the person he was with me," she argues, though less passionately now. "He wouldn't lie like that."

"Wouldn't he?" I murmur.

Her shoulders slump. She looks away.

"Doesn't feel good, does it?" I ask. She's quiet. "So take your emotions and multiply them by a thousand, and that's how I'm feeling."

"Am I supposed to feel sorry for you?" Lindsey snaps, red

slashes forming along her cheekbones. "Am I supposed to regret my relationship with Ethan? It's not my fault he was married. I fell in love with him. Love doesn't know boundaries."

"Maybe not," I answer. "But *people* do. Or people *should*. Married people are out of bounds. At least, they should be for any decent person."

"Have you never broken the rules?" Lindsey asks now, and her young face is weary. "Have you never done something you should be ashamed of? In business? Life? Anything?"

I've been cutthroat at work at times, but never unethical. When I was in high school, I dated a couple of guys at the same time without telling them, but that's as far as it went. And I was just a kid.

"No, actually," I reply. "I've tried to live my life with grace. And I think I have."

"Oh Jesus," Lindsey says, and the doubt is very clear in the air. "Whatever."

"It's true. You *decide* to be a good person," I argue. "It's what I teach my kids. Maybe no one taught you that."

She rolls her eyes. "I know all the cliché sayings. Integrity is what you do when no one is watching. Yada, yada."

"They're not cliché sayings," I say slowly. "They're true. Listen, last year I was at a conference, and the CEO of a very prominent cosmetics company came on to me. He's distinguished, powerful, sexy. And yes, as a woman, I recognized his appeal, but as a *wife*, I never even considered that an option. Ethan would never have known, but *I* would have. That's what integrity is."

Lindsey lifts an eyebrow now. "You never even entertained the idea? Not for one second?"

I pause, thinking. It had been flattering. It had made me feel sexy and desired, something that I now realize we were lacking in our marriage. I was too busy to even realize before, but I'd felt unsatisfied, unwanted, and so had he. The difference between us, though, is lying on the bed in front of me.

My blood is personified fury and it pulses through me, flooding me, and I have to be oh-so-careful, because I hate this girl, I'd like for her to die, and she's tied up on my bed, and I could do it. I could end it.

I'm on the edge of being a monster, and I've got to pull myself back.

I breathe deep.

"No. I never considered it," I say truthfully and with an air of forced calm. "I took a vow to be faithful to Ethan. And I've never wanted to break it."

But I want to break you.

Lindsey rolls her eyes again. "You must be a very boring person."

The anger flares in my temple, like a flash of light. I fight it off. *No, don't go there. Breathe.*

"Why? Because I have principles?" I put a purposeful smirk on my lips. She's beneath me. She's not worth it.

I eye her as her skinny ankles push against the restraints.

"Are you telling me . . . honestly . . . that you've never felt guilty for pursuing Ethan?"

She's the one pausing now. She blinks and then answers.

"I know you want me to say I did, but honestly, no, I didn't. I didn't allow myself to go there. I knew what I wanted, and that was Ethan. I wasn't going to let anything stand in the way of that."

"Fuck you," I spit. "Here I am, trying to believe that deep down, you might be a good person, but you have no sense of guilt or shame whatsoever."

"I'm not a bad person," Lindsey insists, just as thunder shakes the house and branches blow into the shuttered windows.

I'm not sure what is louder, the storm or my fury. The candles flicker around me, hauntingly, and I feel like my sheer anger can extinguish them.

"I didn't try to hurt you," Lindsey says softly.

"You also didn't care if you did," I clarify, and lightning lights up my face, turning my arms silver.

Her gaze drops. "No, I guess I didn't."

"You've got a lot of growing up to do, little girl." I shake my head. "My teenage daughter has a better sense of morality than you do, by far."

"Well, I guess that's because she was raised by Saint Tessa." Lindsey's smirk is more of a sneer, and it's ugly.

"I'm no saint, but I do try hard to be a good person. You should try it sometime." I've got to get out of here before I'm truly tempted to cross the line, to hurt her, and I won't be able to come back from it.

I head for the door, but Lindsey stops me.

"Hey."

I turn, forcing my feet to stay in place. "Yes?"

"Ethan had a secret email account."

My heart starts to race. "Oh?"

He didn't just have a secret account on All the Fish? Even as I think about it, though, I realize I'm being naïve. He had to have an email to tie it to.

Lindsey nods. "Whoseyourdaddy@gmail.com."

"Who's your daddy?" I laugh. "That's . . . no." That's too tacky. That's not Ethan.

But Lindsey is nodding.

"If my phone has a signal, look it up. He probably uses the same password as he does for everything else."

She's right about that. Ethan uses one password for everything.

I pick up her phone, and she does have one flickering bar. I ignore the two additional texts that have come in from Ethan.

Has Tessa tried calling you?

What have you said?

He's trying to cover his tracks, protect his own ass.

Trepidation makes my fingers heavy as I wait for the webpage to pull up, as I enter his log-in credentials, and then . . . as the inbox loads.

Son of a bitch. She wasn't lying. There are dozens and dozens of emails between Ethan and Lindsey, and from the All the Fish website. But then . . . I notice something else, something recent, something that makes my eyes widen and my stomach drop to the floor.

Lindsey isn't the only one.

"What?" Lindsey demands, and I can't answer. I can't form the words. Instead, I turn and walk out, her phone in my hand, as I process this sharp new betrayal.

Ethan was fucking around on both of us.

eighteen

LINDSEY

After hearing nothing from Ethan for two days, he finally texts me midmorning.

Hey, stranger! You up for lunch?

I'd been starting to think I'd really scared him off. I had tried not to be bothered, but I was. He thought I was pregnant, and he bailed.

Maybe. I take lunch in an hour.

He tells me where to meet him, but when I leave work and head for the restaurant, I get another idea. I'll surprise him at his job site.

I pull to a stop a little down the road and watch Ethan striding around his site, in boots and a hardhat, and my belly churns, down low. He looks sexy, so in charge. He turns to speak to someone, and the man nods and leaves.

I text him.

I'm here.

He pauses, staring at his phone, then slowly looks up, around him.

Down the road. I thought I'd surprise you.

He cocks his head and sees my car, parked on the side of the road. He smiles but quickly responds.

You can't really be here.

No one will see me, I assure him. *I just wanted to see you in your natural habitat.*

Is it everything you hoped it would be? ☺

I laugh. *And more.*

Give me a minute.

He disappears into the building. I wait, growing antsier by the minute, until my passenger door opens and he drops into the seat next to me. He'd gone around the block and come up behind so that no one would see him.

I ignore my resentment about that, that he has to sneak

around to see me. But there will be a time when this won't be the case. I have to put in my dues.

"Drive," he says simply. I drive to a nearby parking lot, where Ethan grabs me roughly and kisses me.

"God help me, that was exciting," he says against my neck. He scrapes his teeth against my skin, and reaching over, I feel how hard he is. He liked the idea of a close call, of the possibility of being seen.

"You're so naughty." I giggle, rubbing at the hardness.

"You made me this way."

I want to have sex, but the space limitations in the car prohibit it. So I do the next best thing. I please him with my mouth.

When I'm finished, I wipe my lips daintily, and he groans, pulling me to him.

"You're the most impossibly sexy creature in the world," he tells me. I still taste him in my mouth, and I kiss him so he can tell. He twists his tongue with mine, and soon, we both taste like him. But then, his phone vibrates against my leg. I ignore it, but he doesn't.

"Damn it," he mutters. He gently pushes me away and reaches for his phone, while I pretend to not be annoyed.

"Hello?" he says, rubbing a circle on my shoulder blade. I lean into his hand, like a cat being adored. "Oh, hey, babe."

I sit up straight. It's his wife.

I can hear her through the phone, pleasant and conversational. "I missed you this morning. You got up early. What time will you be home? Can you come to Ava's art show with us? Good, can't wait. Love you."

"Love you, too," he answers before hanging up. He looks me in the eye right after.

"Sorry," he tells me gruffly. It's awkward, and we both know it. "Listen, I'm playing a part right now. That's all. I always answer her calls. If I stopped, she'd wonder why."

"It's okay," I lie. "I get it." I don't. "She has you on a short tether."

He glances at me. "Not really," he says. "Sometimes I feel like she doesn't notice me at all."

"Where were we?" I ask brightly, reaching for him again. But he shakes his head.

"I'm sorry, Linds. I've gotta go back. They'll be wondering where I am."

I'm annoyed, but he just called me Linds. A new nickname. He feels closer to me now. That has to be enough. For today, anyway.

I smile and grab his hand, holding it while I drive.

"So Ava's an artist?"

He nods. "Yeah. She paints."

"That's amazing. I bet your kids are all talented."

"In their own ways," he agrees.

I pull the car up to the curb by where I was before.

"Where is her show?" I ask. His eyes cloud for a second.

"You can't come," he says uncertainly. "You know that, right?"

"Of course. I was just wondering. If it's a big deal or something."

"Oh," he says, sounding relieved. "It's at the arts center. They're highlighting local high school artists."

"That's really amazing," I tell him, and kiss him softly on the mouth. "Enjoy tonight, Daddy. Be proud!"

He smiles, gets out, and walks the long way around the block once again, to hide his interaction with me. My gut twinges, and I ignore it to the best of my ability.

I can't focus on his hesitation to include me in his life just yet. I have an art show to prepare for.

nineteen

TESSA

As I hold Lindsey's phone, staring at the other woman Ethan has been talking with, I have two revelations.

1. Lindsey has a signal again, for now.
2. I have the upper hand. She has no idea about this other woman. It's irony in its purest form.

My life is a swirl of nightmares.

I take a deep breath and focus on the one at hand. Lindsey's phone burns my hand, the implications it contains fiery hot. My husband wasn't just in a relationship with one other woman. He was in a relationship with two, that I know of. Maybe more, who the hell knows at this point?

I fucking hate him. I love him and I hate him, and I want to kill him, and I risked my entire life confronting a mistress when she doesn't even mean that much to Ethan?

What kind of man would do this? What kind of man would

hunt for a new mistress even as he is still fucking the original, all while still fucking his wife?

Is he a psychopath? A sociopath? How could I not have seen this? What is wrong with him?

I scan the emails from Amyisahottie and see he was sexting her via email. Bile rises in my throat at the thought of my husband with someone with a tacky name like that. . . . But it doesn't appear he has met her in person yet.

Is he stringing her along, waiting to see if he needed to replace Lindsey? Maybe he really just wants a plaything, and Lindsey is trying to get too serious? He made Lindsey fall in love with him, and he views her as disposable. Unbidden, I feel a rush of pity for Lindsey. The young, naïve, disposable Lindsey.

This whole time, I've wanted an answer to one main question . . . one unthinkable question. What does Lindsey have that I don't?

But now, it seems that it wasn't the right question in the first place.

The right question is . . . what is wrong with my husband?

My heart pounds and my stomach drops. I feel like I'm going to be sick, violently ill, in fact. But at the very least, from what I can see, he has only been physically unfaithful with Lindsey. I don't know about the past, but I can't dwell on that. The present is where I need to be, and the present is currently in my bedroom.

And what the fuck am I going to do with her now?

As if on cue, Lindsey calls out to me.

"Tessa!" I scowl in her direction, and she calls again. "Tessa!"

I walk to the room woodenly. "What?"

"If you let me go, I won't say a word about this."

"Oh, yeah? And where are you going to go in this storm?"

As if to emphasize my point, the wind howls even louder, shaking the window and the shutter in front of it.

"I'll say I'm a stranger," Lindsey offers. "I was just on this street, my car broke down, you took me in."

"Right," I say.

"I've been around your family before," she says with an off-handed indifference that prickles my skin and makes me temporarily forget the other woman.

I lift an eyebrow. "When?"

"Plenty of times." The smile that stretches across her dry lips is eerie in the flickering candlelight.

"Are you stalking us?" I ask, and my heart beats faster. She's known about us for almost a year. She could've done *anything* in that time.

"I've bumped into you," she answers, "so you can't really call it stalking."

"Did you *bump into* us on purpose?" I ask carefully.

She shrugs.

"When else?"

"Hmm, well, I took Connor's football team a cooler full of Gatorade once when I was Ethan's 'assistant.'"

She looks pleased with her cleverness, and I fight to push back the irritation boiling inside me that she was that close to my son.

"Did you talk to Connor?"

"Only a few times."

Connor knows about this woman? Does he remember her? Did he suspect anything? My fucking kid? *She had the nerve to get near my fucking kid?*

I clear my throat and force my wooden tongue to move. "Does Ethan know?"

"I told him afterward."

"And what did he say?"

"Well, there wasn't really time for words, if you know what I mean," she answers.

"Distraction with sex," I say, shaking my head, and she smiles, realizing I'm finally getting it.

My fingernails curl into my fist, biting into my flesh enough to burn. I want to punch her in the face, over and over and over, until it turns bloody and mashed. But I maintain my calm. I won't allow her to do that to me again.

"Ava is so pretty," she says now. "You must've looked a little like that when you were young. Can you remember back so far?"

My blood boils for a hundred different reasons, including her insults and her refusal to feel guilt. Doesn't she realize that I need her to feel culpable?

"When did you see Ava?" I ask instead, forcing myself once again to remain calm. Ava is fine; Connor is fine. She can't hurt them. They are far from here.

"She's sweet," Lindsey continues, as though she hadn't heard. "You know, it's surprising. You've taught them *so* much, but maybe you should teach your kids not to talk to strangers. They really aren't very careful."

I fight to control my temper. I fight the urge to ask questions. She won't tell me the answers, anyway. She's baiting me. It's possible that this is just bullshit, and she's simply trying to get a rise out of me.

"Hey, Tessa?" Her voice lilts at the end. My eyes narrow. "Look in the side pocket of my purse."

Her tone is sickeningly sweet, like she is going to give me a gift, but I know it's anything but. I don't want to look. But I have to know.

I pick up her worn pink purse and unzip the side pocket. I lift out a delicate silver chain, an anklet with a simple heart on it. Ethan had given it to Ava last year for Christmas. She had been heartbroken when she'd lost it.

And here it is . . . in Lindsey's purse.

twenty

LINDSEY

It's hard to find a parking spot. There are a bunch of proud parents here, all of them wearing bright, shiny smiles. I sit in my darkened car, watching. I don't see Ethan's family. I wonder if they may already be inside.

I check my lipstick in the rearview mirror. Perfect. I smile at myself. Perfect.

I lock my car and then stride confidently into the arts center.

It is swarming with parents and proud high schoolers, and I make my way to the sidelines, positioning myself with my back to the wall, my eyes on the crowd, scanning it for Ethan's face.

"Pardon me." Someone bumps into me. He smiles at me. His hair is thinning on top, but he's still attractive. "Busy, isn't it?"

I nod, swallowing. God, don't let him know the Taylors. I glance at his hand. He's ringless. A divorced dad, probably.

"It's a madhouse," I say, more comfortable now. He probably doesn't hang out with Ethan and Tessa. Not without a wife. Couples tend to flock together.

"Do you know one of the artists?" he asks. I can read his thoughts. *I'm too young to have a high schooler.*

"Yeah. A family friend. You?"

He beams. "My son. He's something else. That's his stuff." He gestures to the opposite wall where charcoal pictures hang, well-lit by the spotlights.

"He's talented," I tell him honestly, studying the drawings. "He captures emotion so well."

A picture of a girl crying catches my eye, and the man notices.

"I like that one, too," he says. "Jasper sees everything. Even things people don't want him to."

Over his shoulder, the faces of Ethan and his wife come into focus, and I startle, then position myself in front of the man so that I'm hidden from their sight. I watch them walk past, Tessa's arm linked through Ethan's.

A flare of hot jealousy shoots through me. The man keeps talking to me, and I pretend to listen, all while watching Tessa and Ethan. They stop and admire a group of paintings, and then their daughter bounds into focus, hugging them both excitedly. Her arms link with theirs, connecting them all in a tight chain.

A family moment.

My throat tightens up while I watch them; I'm an outsider.

Ethan's arm lifts and drops onto Tessa's shoulders, a movement so familiar and intimate. She leans into him, something she's clearly done a thousand times before. They are a well-oiled machine, and I feel nauseous.

I excuse myself, suddenly needing to move, to breathe. Why

am I doing this? I weave through the crowd and browse the art in separate rooms, trying to work up the courage to go back and see more of the exchange between Ethan and his wife.

I'm staring at a painting of a giant fuzzy peach when I hear it . . . Ethan's laughter. I'd recognize it anywhere. My head jerks up, and there he is. Across the room.

He doesn't see me, and he's no longer with Tessa. Instead, he's with a strange woman close to his age. She's in a black pant-suit and has a sleek brunette mom bob. I move, blending in with the nearest group, and keep watching.

He leans in as he talks to her, listening intently when she answers, then throws his head back in laughter. She laughs, too, and touches his elbow, stepping closer to him, and it sure as hell looks like he's enjoying it.

My eyes narrow. She must be the mother of another child. But where is Tessa? I look around. Not in this room.

Ethan and the woman keep talking, and it's like they think they're the only people in the room. Their eyes are locked on each other, and my heart starts pounding. *Who is she?*

She tosses her hair out of her face, and I can feel electricity between them from here. This can't be right. *I* am the only one for him. Aren't I?

But I could swear he's flirting with her. Right before my eyes.

Then, Tessa appears.

Ethan is unfazed and doesn't miss a beat. He just takes a step back and smiles at his wife. The woman he was talking to greets her, and all goes back to normal. He's a family man, once again.

What the hell just happened?

Nausea bubbles in me again, and I bolt. I zip through the

throng of people and find a restroom, rushing straight to a stall. I heave for a moment, but I don't actually vomit. I wait, taking deep breaths, trying to calm myself.

I don't know what I expected when I came here. I knew *she* would be here. I just wasn't expecting to see him so comfortable with other women.

And the way he interacts with his wife . . . I guess I was hoping to see some distance between them, some coldness. But there wasn't any.

So he's either a good actor or he actually loves his wife. So where does that leave me?

The door opens and closes several more times before I'm finally ready to leave my stall. I wash my hands, and as the water warms up, another stall opens.

Ava Taylor comes out and goes to the sink next to me. My heart skips a few beats, and I soap my hands again to stall for time.

"Are you an artist?" I ask her, as though I'm just a friendly stranger.

Ava glances at me, then smiles. "Yeah. I guess."

"What's your name? I'll look for your stuff out there."

"Ava Taylor."

She rinses her hands.

"Are you enjoying the art?" she asks me with a composure and maturity I wouldn't expect from a teenager. She dries her hands with a paper towel, and I reach around her to grab some for myself.

"Yeah. You guys are really, really good. Hey, Taylor. That name sounds familiar."

She grins again. "Well, my mom is on the PTA, and my

dad . . ." She rolls her eyes. "Well, all the women on the PTA are in love with him." She laughs and gives me a sideways glance as she tosses her paper towel in the trash. "Are you one of them?"

Yes. I blink. "No."

She laughs again. "Well, have a good night," she says as she turns to leave.

"You, too," I call after her.

So, apparently, Ethan is popular among the ladies. What I saw was nothing more than a PTA mom hitting on him and him handling it with grace. I should've known.

I start to grab the door handle, but something shiny catches my eye. A silver chain with a heart, too big to be a bracelet but too small to be a necklace. It wasn't there a minute ago. It must've fallen off Ava's ankle.

Bending, I pick it up. It's diamond encrusted. I don't think I even have a piece of jewelry this nice, and I'm more than a decade older than her.

I should follow her and give it back, but I can't risk Ethan seeing me.

And honestly, I want it. What if Ethan gave it to her? Then . . . it's almost like he's giving it to *me*. It would be like I have a piece of him with me always.

I slip it into my purse.

I open the door and scan the hall. It's clear. Ethan isn't in sight. I head for the front doors of the school and burst through them into the fresh night air. I walk toward the parking lot and immediately trip—a boy sits, feet out in front of him, on the curved stones outside of the school.

"I'm sorry," I tell him as I right myself. "I wasn't paying attention."

"It's okay." He shrugs. He's got a sketchbook and charcoal in his hands. I peer at his pad and see a man and woman on the page. As it comes into focus, I almost gasp.

It's Tessa and Ethan.

I remember the stranger I was talking to and how he said his son sees things other people don't.

"What a beautiful picture," I tell him. "May I?"

He nods and hands it to me. On the page, Ethan's hand is slipped into Tessa's pocket, and she's looking up at him with an expression of utter joy, her eyes filled with love.

A lump forms in my throat, and I can't seem to swallow it.

"It's beautiful," I manage to say, handing the drawing back. "Thank you."

I turn and walk to my car alone, but the expression on Tessa's face in that drawing haunts me for the rest of the night.

Regardless of what Ethan thinks, that's a woman who loves her husband. I just have to pray he doesn't realize it.

twenty-one

TESSA

"So, you were at the art exhibit?" I ask incredulously, as I slip my daughter's anklet into my pocket. Ava had been so upset when she'd lost it that night. "Why?"

She shrugs. "I don't know. I wanted to feel like I was a part of his life."

"*My* life," I tell her. "Did Ethan know you were there?"

She looks smug now, as much as she can with her clown mouth and mussed hair. "I found him when he went to the restroom."

Bile rises again, and I swallow it back.

"You found him while he was with his family? While Ava and I were just in the other room?"

"You were oblivious," she says, almost derisively. "You were only focused on Ava. You didn't even notice he was gone."

That wasn't true. It's coming back to me now . . . he did seem to be gone for quite a while that night, and I remember noticing. I'd thought at the time he'd had an upset stomach, and

167

then I'd found him standing with Molly Thompson, the insipid president of the PTA.

"What did you do?" I ask quietly.

"We fucked in a supply closet," she says simply. "Then I went out the back way, and he returned to you. Smelling like me."

I shudder. He'd held my hand on the way out to the car. In fact, he'd held my hand that entire night. I'd felt so close to him that night, and it had been a lie.

"You fucking whore," I say before I can stop myself. "And you think you're not like your father? You really think you're not a home-wrecker?"

She gazes at me, her eyes like shiny pebbles.

"Ethan had a choice, too, you know," she points out. "He knew you were in the other room, and he chose to sneak away to have sex with me. Did he kiss you that night, Tessa? Just think of what else he was doing with that mouth."

My veins turn to ice, because he had kissed me in the car. Long and hard, and I had welcomed it. I had no way of knowing he was hot and bothered because of her, not because of me at all.

I'm so stupid.

"This isn't about him right now. This is about you. Trust me, wherever Ethan is right now, he's beside himself, worrying that he's going to lose everything. He knows you aren't worth it."

"Does he?" she asks, intent on upsetting me. "It never seems to bother him . . . the risk of losing you. In fact, it didn't seem like he cared. He answered phone calls from you when I was right there next to him, even when I was *going down on him*, Tessa. Seems to me, he didn't really care."

That's a dagger to my heart. "Fuck you."

"Fuck *you*."

We thrust and parry, two fencers trying to draw blood.

Outdoors, thunder cracks violently, and lightning flashes on the bedroom walls, coming in beneath the shutters. The earth rumbles with the storm, and I can feel the electricity in the air.

"I have to use the bathroom," Lindsey says now, almost politely.

I stare at her, at the urine-soaked sheets. She follows my gaze and rolls her eyes.

"I don't have to *pee*," she clarifies.

Oh.

"I don't care," I decide. "The mattress is already filthy."

"You're going to make me take a shit on your bed and then lie in it?"

I nod.

"What is your point here?" she demands. "You want to degrade me?" She motions to the smeared lipstick on her chest. "You already did that. You asked for the truth? I gave it to you. What more do you want?"

"I want you to be sorry," I state quietly.

"But I'm not," she says, just as quietly. "I could tell you I am, but I'm not. I love Ethan. I can't help it. And I'm not sorry about it."

"How can you love someone who doesn't love you back? He was never going to leave me for you, Lindsey. Help me understand," I urge her. "Because I don't."

Lindsey presses her lips together and, again, just states, "You'd never understand."

I exhale shakily. We're not getting anywhere and maybe never will. What will I do then? It hadn't occurred to me that she might not be sorry. That I couldn't *make her be sorry*.

"You're unconscionable," I tell her.

"Maybe."

She doesn't believe it, though. I see it on her proud face. She's still arrogant.

"Did Ethan ever say my name when he was fucking you?" she asks me, eyes shining.

"You wish."

"He said he couldn't do certain things with you because you're too much of a prude."

"That's ridiculous," I snap. "And so far from the truth."

Ethan and I have always had an amazing sex life. It only slowed down in the past couple of years, particularly in the past year, and the reason is right in front of me.

I stare at her.

"Did Ethan tell you he was paying my rent?"

I freeze, and she laughs.

"I guess he didn't. Looks like I wasn't the only one lying, was I?"

"I'm quite aware that Ethan was lying to me," I tell her through my teeth. I'm afraid that if I stop gritting them, I'll lose control. I might even kill her. The urge to get violent is suddenly paramount and hard to resist. It's almost scary. I've never been a violent person, but in this moment, I can visualize slamming her head into the wall, watching the blood spray. I swallow. "But I still look over all our bank accounts. I would've seen that."

"He didn't want you to find out." Lindsey yawns, her mouth opening wide. "So he attached a new credit card to his business accounts."

My heart slams against my chest. I've never looked in his business accounts because he's always been scrupulous with them, with the numbers. He never wanted to chance an audit, so it never occurred to me he might use it to hide something. The anger is clouding my vision, and I almost see double. I take a step away from her so I'm not temped to hurt her.

"He wanted me in a safer neighborhood, and I couldn't afford it myself," she answers, shaking her head. "He also got me a dog. He was worried about my safety."

"You don't seem like a dog person," I point out.

"Oh, I am. And you already know my dog," she continues, an iciness in her eyes. "He was yours."

twenty-two

LINDSEY

I find myself once again outside of the Taylor house. My bare feet sink into the damp sand, and I reassure myself that I'm not crazy. I'm not a stalker. I just want a glimpse of Ethan. I want to see what he's doing when he's not with me. I want to compare *her* Ethan with *my* Ethan.

I linger close to the bluffs as I see someone jogging on the beach a few hundred yards away. I think for a minute that it might be Ethan, but as the form draws nearer, I see it's actually Tessa.

What the hell?

For a fraction of a second, it makes me self-conscious. Since I've started dating Ethan, I've stopped going to the gym. He uses up all my spare time. I run my hand over my belly and let the worry go. It's still flat, still tight. I'm still young; I don't have to work hard to look good. Tessa, on the other hand, *has* to work out.

She stretches for a minute at the bottom of the wooden

stairs leading up to her home, and I shrink even farther back into the bluffs. I'm wearing a brown jacket for just this purpose, to blend in. It works. She doesn't notice me.

Her face is red, and sweat has dampened her hair.

A dog sits behind her, an old German shepherd with a white muzzle. It moves a little stiffly as it stands up, and she bends to pet it.

She picks up a stick and throws it down the beach.

"There you go, Duke," she says. "Go get it, old man! Bring it up to the porch."

She heads up the stairs while Duke doggedly chases the stick. It takes him a while, but he retrieves it, intent on pleasing his master. Dumb dog.

He's old. He doesn't need to be chasing after something on her whim. She doesn't deserve this dog. It's probably Ethan's.

As Duke walks slowly back toward the steps, I fish in my pocket for half of a Pop-Tart I know is there. I hold it out to him, hesitant. He's a German shepherd, after all. They aren't known to be receptive to strangers. But he eyes me warily, before dropping his stick and taking a step toward me, to see what I have in my hand.

"Here, Duke," I coax, and he tilts his head because I know his name. "It's okay, boy. I have a treat. Come here."

And to my surprise, he does.

I gently give him a bit of the blueberry pastry, and he sniffs for more.

"Come on, then," I tell him. "Let's go get more."

He's putty in my hands now. He follows me diligently back to my car, intent on one thing: the treat in my hand.

I open the back door and toss the treat onto the back seat.

Despite his age, he jumps in after it. When I get in the driver's side, he's sitting on the console, eager for a car ride.

"Good boy," I tell him. He's making my car smell like damp dog, and I drive away before someone sees us.

What the hell am I going to do with him now?

I've just taken Tessa's dog. I can't take him back to the apartment; Ethan would see him. Damn it. I didn't think this through.

I drive around for a while. Duke is happy just staring out the window, and for a second, I envision keeping him. But there's no way. Ethan can't know what I've done.

I look up the nearest animal shelter on my phone, and steeling my heart, I drive there and drop him off.

"I found him on the road," I lie through my teeth to the nice lady inside. "I didn't want him to get hit by a car."

She pets him and scans his neck. "Hmm, he doesn't have a chip," she says, disappointed. "He looks pretty old. It wasn't as common years back. Thank you for bringing him in. Do you want to leave your name so you can call and check on him?"

I shake my head quickly. "Oh no. That's okay. I can tell you'll take care of him."

"Well, he's a senior dog, so he'll adopt out slower. But we'll do our best."

Duke watches me with deep, soulful eyes as I leave him, and I know what he's thinking.

Liar.

I am. I feel bad about it, but it's too late now.

I call Ethan a little while later.

"Can I call you back?" he asks, distracted. "Our dog has wandered off, and I need to find him before Tessa gets home. She'll freak out otherwise."

"Of course," I tell him, so understanding. "Of course. I hope you find him."

I picture Duke's soulful eyes and tense up. He'll find a home. Anyone would love him.

He's a senior dog, the lady had said. I cringe and put that out of my mind. I don't know why I did this. I just wanted to take something that was hers. Something she loves.

You're already taking her husband, I tell myself, but I know I'm not. Or not yet, anyway. He hasn't left her. Yet.

Ethan comes over later in the evening, and I hand him a beer.

"Did you find your dog?" I ask, already knowing the answer.

He shakes his head ruefully.

"No. Tessa is upset. She was in the shower when he wandered off, and she's pissed that one of us didn't let him in."

"That's hardly your fault," I point out.

"He's never wandered off before," Ethan says now. "He likes to stand on the beach for a few minutes in the morning, and then I let him in. It's what we do every day. Except today."

I try to soothe him in the only way I know how. I kiss his neck, and then I pick up his hand and kiss his palm. But he's not into it.

"I'm sorry, babe," he tells me. "I'm just distracted."

He gets up and gets another beer, gulping it down.

"Listen, why don't you call some of the shelters around your house?" I suggest. "Maybe someone found him."

Ethan's eyes light up. "That's a great idea. Thank you!"

Except the shelter he's at is nowhere near Ethan's house. He'll never think to call it. Damn it. I picture the look on Duke's face as I walked away.

"Maybe call shelters a little farther from home, too," I add. "Dogs can travel pretty far."

I walk him out to the walkway, and a group of teenagers stands in the parking lot, blasting a car stereo. I shake my head. "I hate this area. So many thugs."

Ethan glances at the kids. "They don't look bad," he chuckles. "Just teenagers."

"You haven't seen them all," I tell him. "Especially at night. It's kind of unsafe here, but it's all I can afford."

"Keep your doors locked," Ethan advises, and I'm kind of disappointed he doesn't show any more concern. "And don't walk in the parking lot at night alone if it bothers you."

I nod. "Of course not. I'm just looking forward to graduating so I can get something better."

I wait, half expecting him to volunteer to help pay rent on something nicer. But he doesn't. He's too focused on finding his dumb dog, and for a moment, I feel satisfaction knowing that he won't.

He should've offered to help me. It's the decent thing to do.

I wave as he drives away, knowing full well that he's not going to find his dog tonight.

twenty-three

TESSA

"Ethan gave you Duke," I repeat, staring at the monster in front of me.

She nods. "I didn't want him, but Ethan wanted me to be safe."

"So he gave you my dog." I don't believe her.

"German shepherd? Going white around the muzzle?" she asks, staring at me pointedly. "He likes my bed. But then, so does your husband. We've had sex in yours, too, but he likes mine better."

My eyes spit fire as I narrow them. "We've had Duke since he was a puppy," I say stiltedly. How could Ethan have given him to her?

"I know." She nods. "That's why he gave him to me. He didn't want to lose him again. He said you were careless."

My stomach hits the floor. Duke was *my* guardian, *my* protector. He was glued to my side, until I came home from work one horrible day and Ethan said that Duke was gone, that they

179

had looked everywhere and couldn't find him. How the hell was that *my* fault? Ethan always let him inside after my run, after Duke played outside for a while. He liked it that way. It wasn't my fault.

"He took me to Bermuda to console me after we lost him," I tell her, and I feel so lost now. "He wouldn't purposely give him away and then do that."

Lindsey shrugs. "Maybe he used it as a way to hide the other stuff he was doing with me. He wanted to look like a good guy to you."

It's like someone punches me in the gut. She's right. Ethan gave away my dog to punish me for not paying enough attention, and then he consoled me so that he looked like a hero. What kind of sick, demented person does that?

Part of me wants to confront Ethan right now, and I have to force myself to stop moving toward Lindsey's phone. I'll wait until I have more, and then I'll confront him about everything. All the lies. He's been lying to Lindsey about me—but does he really believe these terrible things about me?

I realize either way, we can't continue. Whether he believes what she says he does or not, we can't continue on a foundation of lies.

Lindsey glares at me.

"I'm not done yet," I remind her.

"Jesus," she mutters. "What else do you want to know?"

"Have you really had sex in my bed?"

She smiles now, a grin that slowly crinkles from ear to ear.

"Yes. We have."

"Liar."

"Why do you ask if you don't believe me anyway?" She lifts an eyebrow.

"You've been in my house before tonight?"

She nods.

"Tell me what it looks like, then."

She stares me in the eye. "Your kitchen has Carrara marble and gray tile floors. The entire back of your house is lined with windows, and you have a veranda with a pretty view. Ethan and I fucked on a chaise lounge while the sun went down."

I seethe. She smiles.

"You asked." She shrugs again. I can't help it. I slap her. Her face snaps to the side, and she barely blinks.

"What else?" I demand.

"Your office is upstairs. Your desk is facing the ocean. He said it triggers your creativity."

"It still doesn't prove that you were actually in my house. Maybe he just described things to you. Or you saw photos," I suggest.

She appears to ponder that. "If only there was a way to prove it," she says slowly. "Like . . . maybe . . . if I'd left something here."

She meets my eyes, and hers are evil.

"Why?"

"Why not?"

"Tell me where it is."

"No."

"Tell. Me."

"No," she answers firmly. "But I'll show you."

"Fuck you."

"*Fuck you.*"

We're back to thrusting and parrying like fencers. I sigh and stomp back out to the kitchen, trying to ignore the dark shadows that lurk in every corner with the power out. We're out in the middle of nowhere. *This* was why I'd wanted Duke in the first place.

Duke.

That bitch has my dog and has possibly been in my house. Maybe they really had fucked in my bed.

I swig the whiskey from the bottle, my palm throbbing from slapping her face.

What could she possibly have left here?

She's got to be lying.

But with every second that passes, it eats at me more. There is something of that little tramp's here in this house. In *my house.* If she's telling the truth, then my husband has lied to me about so much more than I already know.

I grab a butcher knife from the knife block and charge back into the bedroom.

"I'm going to take you out of here, and you're going to show me what you hid. If you try to run, I swear to God I'll stab you in the heart and then tell them that you were an intruder. That you were stalking me."

"And how would you explain the bed?"

I don't answer. Instead, I unfasten both of her hands and then toss her the key for her ankles. I step away and wield the knife. I rock back and forth on my feet, ready to spring if I have to.

She stands up and wobbles. Her ankles are weak now, and her feet are probably asleep.

She steadies herself. "Give me a minute."

"Take your time." I'm glib.

She shakes her ankles and rubs at them. Then she straightens. "Fine. Follow me."

"Don't forget, I'll stab you in the back without thinking about it," I warn her.

"Whatever."

She walks through my house like she owns it, like she knows just where she's going. Like she's been here before.

My heart sinks further and further as we climb the stairs, and then we're in my office. Lindsey walks straight to my big desk facing the wall of shuttered windows and opens the middle drawer.

She pulls out a tube of lipstick from the back corner. A flat burgundy I would never wear. And it's not from Blush. I only wear my own cosmetics.

"It's my signature look," she tells me with a smile, rolling the tube in her fingers and applying it without a mirror. I watch, appalled.

"Why would you stash that in here?"

She looks at me. "Honestly, I don't know. I guess I just wanted something of mine to be here. I knew you'd notice it in your bathroom, but I figured you wouldn't see it in the back of your drawer."

"And Ethan just let you prance around our house un-supervised?"

She looks amused. "He was sticking his dick in me unsuper-vised," she reminds me. "I guess he didn't think I was a problem."

"Go back to the bedroom," I say, my words stilted. I wave the knife.

She steps toward the door.

I'm waiting for her to try to run, but she doesn't. She walks down the stairs, and I'm two steps behind her, careful to not get close enough for her to try to disarm me.

We descend into the kitchen and then walk through the living room as the storm rages on outside and the lightning flashing against Lindsey's face resembles an old movie projector.

We're crossing the threshold of my bedroom when she spins.

Then everything seems to happen in slow motion, the snaps of lightning that flash through the cracks at the bottom of the hurricane shutters capturing us in strange silver moments.

She grabs for me.

I throw the knife so she can't use it against me and I shove her toward the bed. I struggle with her, trying to wrestle her to the mattress and overtake her with my strength.

She bites my arm.

I bite her back.

Lightning flashes against her face, and she's grotesque, crazy, demented.

She rolls away, and I grab her by the bra, trying to yank her back, but it snaps and falls away.

She's topless now, yellow in the candlelight, and she bolts toward the door, but I leap for her, grabbing her ankle. I heave her back and she hits the floor. She falls hard, and then . . . we both stop.

We're both arrested by the sight of a man's silhouette highlighted in the flash of light. At first I think it's Ethan, and my heart pounds in rage. As the lightning strikes again, I see my son's face.

Colton is standing bleary-eyed in the door, staggering . . . and here.

My son is here.

In this nightmare.

twenty-four

LINDSEY

E than was supposed to arrive hours ago.

He hadn't shown up. I've texted him and left him two voicemails, but he hasn't replied. It is so odd, and it's stirred dread in my belly. Because this isn't the first time.

It's happened several times over the past two weeks. He'd been so upset over losing Duke. I really fucked up with that one. I even called the shelter to see if I could get him back, but they'd somehow adopted him out already.

At first, he told me the truth. *I'm sorry. We're putting up posters to find Duke. Tessa is really upset.*

I understood that. It was annoying, but I understood. Then, though, his excuses changed, like he didn't want me to know that he was still babying his wife over the loss of a stupid dog. For days, I got excuses.

I'm sorry, I have to work late. There won't be time to come over.

I'm sorry, I have a meeting. I can't meet you for lunch.

Once upon a time, he'd moved heaven and earth to see me.

He'd rearranged family dinners and called off work. Things felt different now, and I didn't like it.

When Ethan finally calls, he speaks in hushed tones, as though he might be overheard.

"I'm sorry, babe," he says quietly. "I got called away on business. A job collapsed, and I had to come. I'll be gone all weekend. Until Tuesday. I know. I hate it, too."

But he doesn't sound like he hates it. He doesn't even sound upset.

Am I being paranoid? Of course I am.

I answer understandingly, because I'm the understanding girlfriend, not the nagging wife. I am perfect in every way, not old or whiny. *She* gives him grief; I do not.

"It's okay," I assure him. "I'll be here when you get back. I love you."

"Me, too," he answers, as he always does. He never says the words, *I love you, too.* And I don't complain. I know in my heart he means it.

On a whim, I grab my car keys and drive to Ethan's house in the dark. I love coming here, sneaking around, seeing his life. But this time, I have a specific purpose.

I pull up the drive, and the house is dark. Tessa's car sits in the front, sparkling even in the night. Ethan's truck is not here.

He was telling the truth, I decide as I turn my car around and head back down the hill. I feel stupid for doubting him. Maybe he's just been busy lately. I know nothing about the construction industry. Maybe this is just the busiest time of the year.

If no one is in the house, though . . .

I put my car in reverse and go back. I get out and walk quietly around the house to the veranda doors. There is a keypad on one of them, and I punch in the code. I overheard Ethan reminding Connor what it was one day on the phone.

The keypad flashes green, and I'm in. The house is dark. It's elegant and refined. Everything I expected it to be.

Fine things surround me, and I explore each room. I trail my fingers along the Viking appliances and the double-stacked Carrara marble on the kitchen island. The pantry is large and stocked to the brim with food. The dining room has a side bar filled with liquor of every kind and crystal glasses hanging above it.

I find the master bedroom and look through Tessa's clothing. Everything is expensive. I try on a pair of high heels, but of course they're too big. She's an Amazon. They have separate walk-in closets, each paneled in rich wood, with shelves, racks, and drawers.

I sit on the bench in Ethan's and glance at his things. In addition to several pairs of sturdy work boots, he has rows of expensive leather shoes. His shirts are all button-downs, neatly hung. I finger through them and glance at their labels—something called Hemrajani. Since they are all monogrammed on the hem, I assume they are custom-made. They fit him perfectly.

There is a dirty-clothes hamper by the door, and I open it, taking out a shirt. I lift it to my nose. It smells like Ethan. I suck in his scent and take the shirt with me. He won't miss it. I'll wear it to sleep in.

I realize suddenly that I've probably been here too long. If I want to see the rest of the house, I'd better hurry. On my way out of the bedroom, I see a glittering bottle of perfume sitting on a crystal tray on the dresser. I spritz some on my neck, and the very scent is rich, like delicious spiced gold.

I make my way upstairs and find what must be Ava's room. It's scattered and messy but nice. She's got a chandelier in here, the spoiled kid. These kids have no idea how good they have it.

I walk down the hall. At the end, behind double doors, I find Tessa's office. I inhale deeply as I step inside. It smells expensive in here, some sort of oil diffusing in the air. I cross a large oriental rug to sit in her chair, and I rock back and forth in her seat, staring out at the ocean. I watch the waves crash into the shore and listen to the seagulls shrieking.

She has an office at Blush yet feels the need for a lavish workspace at home? She's just as spoiled as her children.

I want to leave my mark here, in this neatly organized place of hers, just something to remind me that she's not so perfect, so bulletproof. I fish in my purse for my lipstick and stash the tube at the back of the drawer, then close it.

That's when I hear something.

A rustling.

A thump coming from downstairs. *Holy shit. Are they home?*

I creep to the hall, but no lights are on. It sounds like drawers are being opened, then closed.

I rush down the stairs, intent on slipping back out to my car, but I have to cross the hall in front of what looks to be a library. It's where the noises are coming from. I glance in and see a dark figure rifling through the desk. He looks up, and his shadowy gaze meets mine.

Fuck.

I make a dash for the door, but he grabs the back of my shirt. I try to wrench away but can't.

"Who are you?" the man demands. We're standing in the moonlight now, and I look up into Colton's face. The oldest.

The hemophiliac. He's supposed to be at college, yet here he is. My heart thuds. He's seen me now.

My cover is blown. Everything is blown.

"I said, who the hell are you?" he demands. He's tall and handsome, skinnier than his muscular brother.

"I'm your mother's assistant," I lie as quickly as the thought comes to me.

Colton eyes me. "You're not Carrie."

I shake my head. "No. I'm not. I'm just a temp while Carrie is out."

"Why are you here?" he asks, firmly now, uncertain whether to believe me. "My parents are in Bermuda. You shouldn't be here."

That answer smacks me in the gut, hard. They're in Bermuda? Together? Ethan's not at work this weekend? He lied to me. That son of a bitch.

"I'm calling the police." Colt decides and reaches for his phone.

"Please don't," I beg immediately. "Please. I'll tell you the truth."

He waits, his thumb on the button, his eyes on my face. "Who are you?"

"Ethan's girlfriend."

There. I said it. It's out in the open. If Ethan wants to lie to me about where he is, the pieces can fall where they may.

Colton staggers back, staring at me. "No way."

"I'm not proud of it," I offer.

"That still doesn't explain why you're here," he says, and he's calmer than I thought he'd be. "Why are you in our house?"

"I left something here." I hold up the shirt I took from Ethan's closet. It's wadded up so Colt won't know it's not mine. "I just wanted to get it."

"My dad told you it was okay to come here alone?" He's dubious, and with good reason.

"Not necessarily," I answer slowly. "I swear, I'm just here to get the shirt."

Colton stares at me now. The shock is heavy in his eyes, and I feel guilty that I've ruined his perception of his father.

"What am I supposed to do with this?" Colt demands suddenly. "If I tell my mom, it will crush her. If I don't, I'm a part of this. I can't believe my dad. This is such bullshit."

"It didn't start out like this," I offer. "Not at all. Your dad is a good man. This all just happened . . ."

"He tripped and his dick fell into you?" Colt is sardonic.

"No. It's . . . complicated."

"No, it's not," he argues. "My father can't do this. He's married! It's not complicated."

"Please don't say anything," I ask. "I know you don't know me, but . . ."

"I *don't* know you. I don't want to know you. What I want is for you to leave. I'll take this up with my dad."

"Please don't," I beg, and my voice is thin now.

"Get out of here," Colton says sharply. "And don't come back. This is my mom's house."

I don't hesitate. I sprint out the door.

"Wait," he calls. I pause, my hand on the handle, and turn hesitantly to look at his grim face. He's tall and lanky, and I see Tessa in him.

"End it," he tells me solemnly. "My mother doesn't deserve this."

I open the door and run.

twenty-five

I push past my horror that my son is here, because Colton can hardly stand, and his eyes are unfocused. I focus on that. There's blood soaked through his jeans. I open my mouth to ask what happened, but he speaks first.

"Who are you?" he demands of Lindsey, and his words are slurred.

"Nobody," Lindsey stammers, but Colt looks to me.

"What's going on, Mama?"

The light is dimming in his eyes by the minute, and he doesn't seem to register the fact that Lindsey is topless, that we're both bleeding, that my clothes are torn. He doesn't understand the situation because he's lost a lot of blood. I can see it.

His vision is tunneling, his pupils pinpoints. He's swaying, and I know I have mere moments.

"Here, Colt." I motion toward the chaise lounge closest to me.

He steps toward me. He's unaware of everything. He just

hears my voice, his mother telling him to do something, so he does it. He focuses on that, on me, to stay afloat.

But he doesn't make it. He falls heavily to the floor and sprawls at my feet. His hand unfurls and rests across my foot, white and limp. I taste blood in my mouth as I kneel next to him and slap lightly at his face, trying to bring him to.

"Colt," I say sharply, but his eyes are rolled back in his head. Only the whites show, and the corners are thick with red tissue and veins.

He's unresponsive.

"Colt." I shake him, a little harder now. "Colt, baby, where are you hurt?"

Nothing.

His head lolls from side to side, and he's so pale. His jeans are torn, and I see a gash in his leg. It's bleeding heavily.

I shake him harder, then check his pulse. It's faint.

"Damn it."

I leap to my feet and sprint for the kitchen. I fling open the fridge door for the blood-clotting factor bags stacked at the back. Thank God the power hasn't been off too long. It's still cool. But it's just one more thing to be pissed at Ethan about. He hadn't left gas for the generator. Without the generator, the factor will go bad, and then where will Colt be?

I grab a bag and the needle kit from the kitchen closet, then run it back to the bedroom.

As I round the doorway, Lindsey is bare-chested but kneeling next to him. She'd torn his shirt into a tourniquet and tied it above his knee, examining the wound with a candle. I'm shocked, but I can't register that right now.

I see something, something dark.

I collapse next to Colt, my knee slamming into the stone.

My fingers feel his wound and find something rough, something rigid.

"Oh my God," I breathe, my fingers curling around it. "It's part of a tree." It's lodged in his leg, and I start to pull it out.

"No!" Lindsey shrieks, and grabs my hand. "Don't. That could be wedged against his artery. That could be keeping him alive. If you take it out, he could bleed to death on the spot."

In horror, I realize she's right. Sweet Jesus. I might've almost just killed my son,

I tear open the needle supplies with my teeth to avoid thinking about that. My fingers are shaking as I try to find a vein, to set his IV. I keep missing the vein. It sinks in deep, too deep. I fish around, trying again. It doesn't work. My hands are shaking too much.

Lindsey pushes my hand away. "Here. Let me. I'm in nursing school. I know how."

She sets the IV with ease and my mind spins. *She's in nursing school, and she's saving my son's life.*

"The clotting factor?" She reaches a hand out. I give it to her, and she sets the flow of the bag, holding it high.

"Do you have an IV stand?"

"Yes, of course."

My legs are rubbery as I get to my feet again and head to Colt's room. There's one behind his door. I grab it and rush back as I hear Lindsey's voice above the wind and the squeaky wheels of the IV stand.

"Yes, yes. We have an emergency. We've got a kid here who needs help . . . damn it." She yells to me, "We don't have a signal."

Her phone must've been close enough for her to grab, and

she tried to call 911. I can't worry about that now. I clear the door, and he's still as a stone.

Lindsey looks up at me. "He's not breathing. I think he lost so much blood he went into shock."

"Colt, please," I beg, as I push, push, push on his chest with all my weight. I press my fingers to his pulse and put my ear over his mouth. She's right. He's not breathing. "Come on. Please."

I don't taste the blood in my mouth anymore. I don't feel the burn of the scrapes on my leg. It all fades away. Only Colt remains. Only Colt matters.

"Please, baby, please," I beg, over and over.

And then I pump his heart for him.

Over.

And over.

And over.

And over.

Then he coughs. I pause, and he's still. Then he coughs again, and mucus splatters onto my shirt. But I don't care.

"Colt!" I clutch him to me, rolling him on his side as he vomits in my lap, then sucks in a heaving breath.

He's breathing.

He's breathing.

I exhale, and my heart is limp.

"Mama," he says weakly, his lips barely moving. "There's a tree down in the road."

He doesn't even know he was dead.

"I tried to come. To come here. But there's a tree down. I had to walk. I tripped on it, a limb tore my leg."

"It's okay," I croon, pushing the hair out of his face and

wondering how he even got to our driveway. "It's okay. You're here now. It's okay."

He's alive. He's alive, and it's all I can think; it's all I care about. Next to me, Lindsey attaches the IV bag to the stand and then steps back.

"I didn't mean to," he mumbles now, his eyes closed and his hands covered in vomit. "I didn't mean to, Mama."

"It's okay," I tell him, rocking my boy. "It's okay. You're safe. You're safe."

But then, a shadowy figure looms over us, and I see Lindsey with the knife in her hand, and I know that was a lie.

We're not safe.

twenty-six

LINDSEY

The hospital lights glare artificially from the ceiling. Their fluorescence turns everything a slight green. No one looks healthy here.

I grab the stack of charts I'm supposed to be working on during this clinical rotation and sit at the nurse's station. But before I start, I check my phone. Logan texted. I smile as I read his words.

> *Mommy, we won our soccer game, and Gramma took me for ice cream!*

I should be the one taking him for ice cream. I mean, what am I even doing here? Nothing is working as it should.

Ethan hasn't called or texted.

It's been a full day since I ran into Colton at their house. I texted Ethan last night, a normal text, and he didn't reply.

Did Colt confront him? Did he call Ethan while he was on

vacation with his wife and demand that he break up with me? Did Colt call *Tessa*?

Maybe they split up. Maybe she left him. My heart leaps at the thought, and I try not to get my hopes up. I couldn't be so lucky. Besides, I wouldn't really want it to happen that way. His kids would never forgive me for being the other woman, and how would that work in the long run? It wouldn't. So I've got to be patient.

I focus on the chart, making my notes before closing it and grabbing another.

A crackling sound comes over the loudspeakers, then an urgent voice.

"Code blue, room four. Code blue, room four."

I leap to my feet because that means *all hands on deck*. Someone's heart has stopped.

I rush to room four, and the room is already frenzied when I step inside. A teenage girl lies on a gurney, pale and limp. Her leg has a gash in it, and she's got a head wound. While someone from the code team starts compressions, someone else warms up the paddles. I rush to wash my hands, and then my training kicks in.

I place pressure on the gash in her leg. The blood is bubbling up through my fingers, and I know it's imperative that we staunch the bleeding as soon as possible.

"Put more pressure on that," a doctor barks to me as he grabs the paddle. Then he yells, "Clear."

We all step away as the girl's body lurches toward the ceiling.

Her leg bubbles and bubbles, a crimson fountain, and I'm certain her femoral artery has been cut. We've only got seconds to fix it.

"Clear!" the doctor calls again, and her chest lurches again.

She slumps back to the table, and we all look at the monitor. Still a flat green line.

The code team continues to work, and I continue to press on the wound, but by the time they call her time of death, I'm covered in her blood. It has soaked through my top and splattered on my pants. My arms are painted with it, streaked from shoulder to wrist. It smells like rust and salt.

I'm motionless, and the blood drips from my fingertips onto the white tile floor. I still don't move.

Long after the room is silent, the sheet has been pulled up over her face, and another nurse tries to reach her next of kin, I stand still at the foot of the bed.

This is the first patient I've seen die. It shook me.

Her toe pokes up from under the sheet, and she's wearing a toe ring and hot pink nail polish. She can't be more than twenty. Her parents are going to be devastated.

I don't want to be here when they arrive, so I rush away. I head to the bathroom, trying to still my pounding heart, and I call Ethan.

He answers.

"Hey," I say, relieved. "We just lost a patient. My first. She was so young."

"That's terrible," Ethan says, and he sounds sincere, if distant. "I'm sorry, Lindsey."

Lindsey

He hasn't called me by name in a while. It's been *babe* for months.

"I mean, I know this is why I want to be a nurse, to help people," I press on, pretending to ignore it. "But it's hard, Ethan. I didn't know it would be this hard."

I realize that I'm crying, and I hadn't meant to be.

"Try to focus on the good you do instead," he suggests. "Try to focus on the people you save rather than the ones you can't. Not everyone is savable, Linds."

Linds. That's a little better.

"I know," I agree. "It's just hard. I'll be all right."

There's silence on the other end of the line, and then he speaks. "I'll come over tonight."

Relief floods me, and love bleeds into my heart.

"Thank you," I say.

We hang up, and I return to the nurse's station. I'm still charting when I hear the wailing an hour later.

It's coming from room four. I swallow hard. The girl's parents must've arrived.

Her mother shrieks and cries, and I've never heard anything so desolate, so empty, so pained. It makes me want to scoop my son into my arms and never let him go.

I call him when I get home, just to hear his voice. Listening to Logan comforts me for a while, but then depresses me when I hang up and I'm in this apartment alone, far from him.

I'd originally used this as a way to get Ethan over to my house, but by the time he arrives, I find that I actually do need him. I need human comfort.

"The look on the mother's face when she came out of that room." I shudder as I sit next to him on the couch. "God. No one should ever have to go through that. It must be the worst thing on earth."

"Losing a child is my worst fear," Ethan says, his face grave. "We've had a few close calls with Colt, and I swear, my life flashed before my eyes. It's terrible. I'm sorry you had to see that."

"Nothing will happen to Colt," I promise him emptily. We both know I don't have the power to keep that promise.

He puts his arm around my shoulders, and we sit together, silently, doing nothing but counting our blessings, that Logan and his children are safe and healthy and strong.

twenty-seven

TESSA

I'm covered in sticky vomit, and I stare up at Lindsey, with Colt in my lap, as she looms above us.

"I can help," she tells me. But she's still holding the knife. I look at it, and she follows my gaze.

"I won't use this if you don't make me," she says, her eyes glittering. She's not friendly, but she's not hateful either. I don't know what to think.

"Why should I trust you?" I'm holding my son in my arms as he drifts in and out of consciousness.

"Your son shouldn't have to pay for your mistakes. Isn't that what you told me?"

I clench my jaw. It was exactly what I'd told her.

"We've got to keep him conscious," she says, peering down. "And we need to warm him up. He's still in shock."

We? There is no *we*. But she's right. I slap at his face. He blinks and shivers but doesn't really stir.

"Can you help me get him into the shower?" I ask. I don't

know why I'm asking. I know I can't trust her, but I'm desperate. And this is my son. As long as he's okay, I don't care what else happens.

She nods, despite her soiled skirt and bare tits, and puts the knife down.

She eyes me, then kicks it away, out of my reach. It skitters across the floor. I couldn't care less about the knife, or even her, in this moment.

Together, we drag Colt through my bedroom and into the bathroom. She limps. She must have hurt her leg in our wrestling match. Her bare breasts brush against my bare shoulder, and it's ironic that the two of us are half-naked, together.

We heave and pull because even though he's thin, my six-foot-six-inch son is over two hundred pounds. But we manage. My shower is a walk-in, and we pull him over the small ledge and lower him onto the stone without disturbing the branch rammed into his leg.

He sprawls on his back, one eye half-open, the other closed.

"Mom?" he moans. He's breathing, though. He's breathing.

I turn on the water, making it hot, but not too hot. Thank God our water heater is gas. He howls in his unconscious state and instinctively tries to roll away, so I drop next to him and hold him still, the water pelting my face.

"It's okay, Colt," I reassure him as my hair plasters to my face. "We have to stay awake. We have to warm you up. It's fine."

He rolls, though, since he's only half-conscious and still attached to his IV.

Lindsey sits by his feet, holding them in place.

The water floods over both of us, soaking us, cleansing us. In this moment, we are the sum of our parts. Two broken, half-naked women with makeup streaking down our faces, with blood on our lips and arms. We are a lesson in irony, a broken moral compass.

Lindsey's legs are splayed around Colt's, her skirt basically in tatters. The word *WHORE* is smeared now on her chest, a bright red badge of who she is and what she's done.

My shirt is torn, my shoulders bare, thick red scratches from Lindsey's fingernails trailing from collarbone to elbow. I've never in my life been so ragged or felt so empty.

"This doesn't change anything," I tell her as I cradle my kid to my chest. "Nothing."

She nods curtly without a word.

"But thank you," I whisper. She looks at me, then looks away. I'm not gracious, and she's not receptive.

Colt stops trying to kick, and she releases his calves. He opens his eyes, and his teeth are chattering.

"Mom?" he asks, as though he's seeing me for the first time tonight. He blinks and looks at our surroundings: the shower, the water, the other woman at his feet. He focuses on her, blinking again.

"It's you," he says, and he's not happy.

Lindsey swallows hard.

I reach up and twist off the water. The silence in the bathroom is deafening as we pull Colt to his feet and wrap him in towels.

"Let's go out to the couch," I tell him. He tries to take a step but falters. Lindsey and I each grab an arm and help him the rest of the way, leaving droplets of water in our wake. Once we have him settled on the couch, I motion to her.

She follows me to the edge of the kitchen. I stare at her. "So how does he know you?"

She has a towel around her shoulders now, and she looks away.

"I saw him once," she admits. "Here."

"Ethan introduced you to my son?" My voice takes on a high pitch that I can't help. That's just . . . I can't deal with that. But she's shaking her head.

"No. He didn't. I came here. I wanted to see if he was lying to me about where he was. He said he was away on business. I came to check. Colton was here."

I think about that. Colt had been out of the house the whole time Ethan was having his affair with this girl. So that doesn't add up. "When was that?"

"When you were in Bermuda."

I want to smirk at her, to crow victoriously, but the look on her face is miserable, utterly dejected, like a dog who's been kicked.

"He *did* lie to you, didn't he?" I ask instead, trying to keep my voice neutral.

She nods, picking up her chin. "Yeah."

"Well, he was in the midst of an affair," I say matter-of-factly, the way I've been trying to think of it all along. It's the only way I can wrap my head around his behavior, the way he was so able to hurt me. "He was in lying mode. It had become a way of life for him. He didn't want to be found out."

She nods curtly again.

"So you met Colton," I remind her, pulling her back to where we were, urging her to continue.

"Yes. I wanted to see what your home looked like, so I let myself in. Colton was here. I'm sorry."

"You're sorry for that, but not for fucking my husband?"

She looks away. "Look, our children are off limits. I should've realized that then, and I'm sorry now. *For that.*"

"For *that*?" I shake my head, disgusted.

"There's no cell signal again," she says, changing the subject. "I tried to call an ambulance."

"You tried to call for help," I correct her. She shakes her head.

"I tried to call for help for Colt. Yes, I would've gotten help, too, but in that moment, I wanted to save your son. He needs help."

"He still needs a hospital, but he says the road is blocked. Lightning must've hit the cell tower." I listen as the storm rages and blows, and I know it's not safe to drive.

"He'll be okay as long as we keep that stick in place. Does he do prophylactic treatments?" Lindsey asks me, and her own teeth are chattering slightly.

"Yes. And those manage the internal bleeds he could get, but if he gets wounded, he always has to infuse clotting factor," I answer. "Luckily I had some here."

"He's in shock, and we're stuck here," she points out needlessly.

"Yeah, until we get a signal and can call for help to have the tree moved. He should be safe now, though. Or safe enough. I'll just have to watch him."

"I'm not going back in that bedroom," she informs me. "I don't care what you try to do to me. It's not happening." She keeps a safe distance from me just to make sure.

I don't even care about her anymore. "I don't care what you do. Just stay away from me." I glance at her. At her nakedness. The irony that she is closer to Colt's age than Ethan's or mine isn't lost on me. My lips press together. "And you should put some clothes on," I add.

"My bag is in the car," she answers, and we both look at the monsoon outside, the rain pelting the house in sheets, pounding against the ground, flooding my yard. I sigh.

"Fine. You can borrow something of mine. You can't sit around naked with Colt here. Go into my bedroom, and in my drawers, you'll find yoga pants and T-shirts. Take your pick."

Her lip curls up, and I know she's thinking about how Ethan supposedly told her that's all I wear. I ignore it.

I check my phone while she's gone. I don't have a signal either. That means I can't call for help if I need it, and I can't get texts from Ethan or the kids. If Lindsey decides to try to hurt me, I'll have to deal with it on my own.

A crack of thunder reverberates through the house, and I feel the floor vibrate. My own shirt is ripped as well, so I follow Lindsey to my bedroom.

It looks like a war zone. The bed is covered in urine and blood. The handcuffs dangle from the head- and footrails, and the bedding is tangled and soiled.

Lindsey watches me from across the room. She's wearing a pair of black yoga pants and a plain pink T-shirt. I notice annoyingly that it's formfitting on me but hangs loosely on her.

I pull open a drawer and grab a clean soft-blue shirt. I take off the torn one, throwing it in the trash, and pull on the new one. She watches me, and I watch her. We're wary, uneasy. Neither of us is going to trust the other. We're two tigers, caged.

"Now what?" she finally asks. There's blood on the side of her face. I don't know if it's hers or mine. She's not friendly, yet not adversarial. Her wrists and ankles are both still a bit bloody, too. I wonder if she's secretly plotting to kill me.

"I don't know," I say shortly.

"You've never held someone prisoner before?" She's sarcastic, bitter. I swallow, and the regret billows in me like the storm outside. I can't believe I've done this. I'm not this woman. I'm in control; I'm impermeable; I'm reliable. *This isn't me.* I've fallen so far from where I should be, from where I normally am.

"This wasn't me," I say, and I don't know why I bother. She shakes her head.

"No, this *is* you," she answers. "You did this."

"As did you," I remind her. "You're not innocent."

"One bad decision shouldn't justify another," she says. She seems absent now, lost in another thought I'm not privy to.

"You can leave. I don't even care anymore," I tell her again.

She stares at me, then looks toward the window. "And how exactly am I supposed to do that?"

I don't answer. I turn and walk away to check on my son. He's what matters.

But he's not in the living room. I scream his name, unsettled, suddenly terrified, and I bolt down the hall.

"I'm in here," he calls weakly.

Colt is in the kitchen, opening a bottle of water. His hands shake, and his face is pale.

"You died," I tell him as I stand next to him. I reach out and touch his arm to feel his warmth, to convince myself that he's okay now. He's cold and clammy, not all that warm.

He stares down at me. "I'm sorry." His voice is thick, syrupy, like his throat is full. "I didn't mean to."

Lindsey steps into the room. She looks at him, and he looks at her.

"You've got to lie back down," she tells him. "You can't dislodge the piece of wood in your leg."

"Why are you even here?" he demands from her, like he's summoning all his strength for this. "I told you to end it with him."

My head snaps back. "You knew?"

Colt's face blanches. "I didn't think you should have to know. You deal with so much already."

I am still as I ponder this. "How long have you known?"

"He saw me that night," Lindsey speaks up from the table. She's folded onto a chair, her legs tucked beneath her. "Not ever again."

"You've known for months," I say slowly, trying to understand.

"Mom, I'm sorry." He turns to me, his hand on my elbow. His fingers are sheer bones. "I didn't want you to get hurt if you didn't have to. I don't know what Dad was thinking. All I know is I talked to him, and he said he was going to end it." He glances at Lindsey, disdain on his face.

She flinches at his words.

"So what is she doing here?" Colt asks. He steps backward, clearly dizzy.

"Let's get you to the couch," I suggest, leading him there. "You've got to stay still." I pull a blanket from the basket and cover his lap. "She was here to see Dad, but he's on his way back from New York."

"Now we're all stuck here because of the storm," Lindsey agrees, backing my story for whatever messed-up reason of her own. "Together."

Colt looks at me, and there is a dark, unspoken understanding in his eyes, as though he remembers the state we were in when he came in and has decided not to mention it.

The whole situation is so messed up that it's unfathomable, something from a movie, something from a nightmare.

I lean in. "Colt, we're giving you factor right now, but you're in shock. You probably won't feel great for a while. As soon as we get a signal again, we'll have that tree moved and get you to a hospital."

"It's not like I haven't gone through this before," he says wryly, and his hands shake so much now that he can't hold the bottle to his mouth. I take it from him, holding it instead. He sips at it, his lips white. "I'm tired, Mama," he says, his pale eyelids closing.

"It's different this time, baby," I tell him. "You've got to stay still. Okay?"

He nods, and I'm scared to allow him to sleep but unable to keep him awake. He is out within minutes, and I pace next to him, keeping a watchful eye on his chest, making sure it stays moving, up then down. Up then down.

From time to time, I pause and kneel to hold his hand. I feel his pulse, erratic but strong. *Okay, it's fine.* I pace again, trying to harness my panic. *He's fine.*

"So where do you think Ethan has really been?" Lindsey asks me finally, through the lightning flashes and the thunder.

I glance at her. "I told you. He's in New York for business."

She looks unconvinced, though. And suddenly, I realize . . . so am I.

twenty-eight

LINDSEY

B ecause of his sweetness with me after I lost the patient, I
didn't tell Ethan that I knew he'd lied about his trip, that
I knew he'd been in Bermuda with his wife.

Besides, how could I? He'd have to ask how I know.

But it burns in me . . . the knowledge that he lied to me,
that he wanted to be with his wife instead of me. He lied to
me. He was supposed to be lying to *her*. It's the one edge I have
over her. That fact causes flames of anguish to rage and rage, but
there's nothing I can do.

He still texts me, still sexts me. He still comes over on most
evenings, and we still get lunches. We still have sex, although
nowadays, it definitely feels like fucking. He came back different
from that trip, somehow, though I can't put my finger on how.
He's more distant. More detached. I don't like it.

"Where are you tonight?" I murmur now, trailing my
hand through his chest hair as we lounge in my bed. Ethan
yawns.

"I'm just thinking about what I have to do tomorrow for work," he answers, distractedly. "I'm sorry."

"Don't be," I say brightly. "We can't stay in fantasyland forever." Yet that's exactly what I was supposed to be for him . . . a fantasy. A break from reality. If that fantasy is marred, there's no reason for him to stay with me. Except for the phenomenal sex. I reach for him again, aiming for an encore. If I can keep him sated, keep him wanting more, it will all be okay.

But he kisses my forehead and rolls away. "Babe, you know I'm an old man," he says as he puts on his jeans. "Sometimes I can't keep up with you."

He used to try, though.

I hide my disappointment. "It's okay," I assure him, wrapping a sheet around myself and standing up.

"Does Tessa want you home?" I say her name with disdain. Ethan glances at me. "Do you have to go so soon? I miss you." I puff my bottom lip out in a pout, but he doesn't notice.

"I'm sorry," he says. "But I promised Connor I'd go to his game tonight."

"Oh. Okay. Make sure you take him some Gatorade."

He glances at me quickly, almost amused. It was such a mom thing to say, something *reality* based, not fantasy. *Stupid.*

"Tessa can't be there," he tells me. "She's working again, so I really need to go for him."

Of course I understand that. He's said Tessa has been working so much that she rarely comes out of her office. The kids need someone to be there for them.

"Colt was going to come, but he can't drive down." He stares at me, waiting for me to say something.

Has Colt said something to him?

I open my mouth, then close it. "Then of course you have to go."

I kiss him on the mouth, reminding him of what waits for him here. He kisses me back, then he's gone. He climbs in his truck and drives back to the other part of his life. The part I don't have a place in.

I knew what I was signing on for. I did. But somehow, I hadn't thought we'd still be in this predicament at this stage.

After he leaves, I'm alone again and restless. I make a vodka with orange juice and sip it, but it doesn't taste right. I look at the carton and see that the juice has expired. I spit it out into the sink and dump the rest.

I look at Tessa's social media updates for today. There's a picture of Connor in his football pads heading out their door. "Big man on campus this year," she captioned it. "Spring football isn't his favorite, but it keeps him in shape!" I'd wondered about that. At least I know that Ethan wasn't lying. He was going to Connor's football game.

I look at Tessa's post from yesterday, a photo of her and Ethan posing together over a giant margarita. "Hubby of the Year!" she said. "Had a long day, so he treated me to dinner!"

Ethan's arm is around her shoulders casually, in the familiar way of a husband. Her eyes twinkle, and she has no idea that the hand draped along her shoulder was buried inside of me the day before. I smile a little at that, but then the idea that he still went home to her kills that short-lived joy.

I dial her number, blocking my own. If an unknown number called me, I personally wouldn't answer. But she does. "Hello?"

she says, as though she's rushed and distracted. I don't say anything. I just wanted to hear her voice. "Hello?" She sounds a little annoyed now. I hang up.

Something urges me on in my head. I don't know why, but I listen to that voice.

I pull on a hoodie and get into my car. I drive to the high school and pay my five bucks to get into the game before I walk to the visitor's side opposite the home bleachers. From here, I can see Ethan and Colt halfway up the stands on the fifty yard line. Tessa is wedged in between them.

He said she couldn't come.

My stomach plummets a little. Why would he lie again? Did he not want me to know he's with her tonight? He's married to her, after all. I know he has to be with her sometimes. Or maybe he *wanted* to be with her tonight, and *that's* what he didn't want me to know.

I pull my hood up so they don't notice me and watch as a kid carrying refreshments comes down their aisle. Ethan stands up and gestures him over. He buys drinks and hands one to both Tessa and Colt, then buys a hot dog. I watch him eat it then slip his arm around his wife again. She leans into him, like she owns him. From time to time, she smiles up at him or laughs at something Colt says. She's very present tonight, very interactive with her family.

They're disgustingly ordinary.

Why would he lie to me? I remember something my mother said to me, and it rings over and over in my head. I wince, trying not to think about it. But it's there all the same.

Lindsey Elizabeth, he'll never leave his wife for you.

God, please don't let my mother be right. I pick up my phone and text Ethan.

I miss you already.

Come over after the game?

I watch him glance at his phone and put it back in his pocket.

He doesn't answer.

twenty-nine

TESSA

Colton moans a little in his sleep as Lindsey jostles his leg. She wraps it in a fresh bandage, and everything in me wants to tell her to get away from him, but yet, at the same time, I'm grateful. I remain silent and sit on the cushion next to him.

He's covered in sweat, his hair plastered to his forehead. I get a cool, wet washcloth and place it on his forehead.

"You're okay," I remind him, even though he can't hear me. I check his pulse to be certain. He's fine. It's there. It's strong.

I exhale.

Lindsey checks her phone again at the table. *Lindsey is sitting at my table.* A muscle in my temple twitches, and I don't know exactly what to do.

"Still no signal," she says to the room, not necessarily to me, but I'm the only one conscious to hear her. "I guess I just assumed you don't have a house line?" She lifts her eyebrow in question.

I shake my head. "No. We got rid of that a couple of years ago. We never used it."

Why am I explaining this to her? I'm annoying myself.

The candlelight flickers, and the shadows morph and bend on the walls. The thunder rolls as rain pounds against the house, and there is endless black beyond the glass. We're trapped in a globe of water and anger and blood.

Lindsey looks up.

"What did Ethan say about me?" she asks now, and her voice is small.

Did she really just ask that? I stare at her, dumbfounded.

"I told you," I answer slowly. I walk to the table and sit down across from her. Her lip is fat from our fight, and there is a shadow of a bruise beneath her eye. "He told me that you were nothing to him."

She is wounded. I can almost hear her heart break, and surprisingly, I don't feel anything. I don't feel remorse, but I also don't feel joy at her pain.

"You know," she says now. "If you were just a better wife to him, he wouldn't have cheated on you."

"With all due respect," I say, and I have no respect for her, "you don't know anything about me or about my marriage. I am a good wife."

"Everyone probably thinks that." She shrugs. "You were buried in your work, always consumed with Colton. You barely noticed if Ethan came or went. If you had been paying attention, you'd have discovered the affair long ago."

I think on that, my belly a hollow log, carved out and empty. I must be in shock, too, because I'm utterly numb now. No emotion whatsoever. And her statement isn't something I haven't considered already.

"I work a lot." I acknowledge the truth from a distance.

"But I end my day at a reasonable hour. I'm always out of my office before Ethan even gets home. I'm there for my kids. My husband always has what he needs. I make dinner almost every night, and we sit down together as a family to eat it. We even put our phones away so we can focus on one another. If Ethan told you otherwise, it simply isn't true."

"He told me that your head was always in the clouds and that you never left the house. That you were a hermit and he worried about you a lot. Because of Colton."

"That last part is true," I tell her. "At least, Ethan did seem like he worried. Truthfully, though, it's not like I've been a fragile wreck. Anyone would be upset and worried in my position."

I refuse to allow anyone to make me think I am fragile. Not about this.

"I've held everything together as best I can," I continue. "I've had two other kids to think about, a career, a husband . . . I'm not Superwoman. I have emotions, but I'm very controlled. I rarely get overwhelmed by them."

"Then how do you explain tonight?" Lindsey asks simply. "And how do you explain the Xanax that you eat like candy?"

So Ethan had told her that, too. Another betrayal. And regarding her questions, I don't have a good answer. She waits for one, though, her head cocked and her skinny hands twisting together on the table.

"Tell me why you did this," she says.

"I don't know," I tell her, even though she doesn't deserve an answer. "In the moment I found out, I had to have answers. It was a blinding need, and Ethan couldn't give them. I also realized that no matter what happens with Ethan and me, I'll carry the baggage of your affair with my husband forever, and you'll get to walk away scot-free. You'll have no repercussions, nothing at all. It didn't seem fair."

"You don't know about my repercussions," she says evenly. "You don't know what it's like to be me."

"No," I agree. "But I know what it's like to be *me*. To be walking through life, minding my own business, and to have a stupid girl set her sights on my husband and try to steal him away."

"Do you really think I acted alone? That he wasn't a willing participant?"

"Of course not," I assure her. "But he'll pay for it. Dearly. You won't."

"I have," she disagrees. "I'm the one he left every night to return to you. To your house, to your kids. I got your castoffs. His leftover time. Do you know what that feels like?"

"No," I answer. "I've never stooped so low to know. And you knew what you were getting into."

"You think you're so high-and-mighty, don't you?" she asks, venom dripping off her words. "You think you're better than me. But you aren't."

"I don't think I'm better than you," I tell her. But that's a lie. "I think you have issues. Issues that make you believe you're only worth this kind of life."

She rolls her eyes.

"I don't know how you imagine my relationship with Ethan," she says, and there is fire in her words. "But he never made it seem like I was second best. He never made me feel like I wasn't worthy of him."

"Yet he left you every night to come home to me. You said so yourself," I point out.

"True. But he didn't want to lose everything he had worked for all of these years. He was trying to find a way out."

I laugh now, a burst of actual amusement. It barks through the kitchen, even above the sound of the rain.

"You're crazy," I tell her. "He was never going to leave me. If he wanted to, he would've. He begged me to stay with him when he texted earlier."

"For the kids," she argues. "For his business. And maybe because you're familiar to him, easy. But I'm going to tell you some things . . . things you'll be surprised to hear. And then maybe you'll change your mind about your husband's good intentions."

She settles a smug gaze upon me, and icy fear envelopes my heart.

thirty

LINDSEY

I'm losing him.

I scroll through Ethan's Facebook page, the recent pictures someone tagged him in from a tailgate party. He was lounging with Tessa, looking perfectly content. His wasn't the face of someone who was planning to leave his wife.

My blood runs cold. I'd never really thought Ethan staying with Tessa was a real option before. I mean, I'm better than she is. I'm younger. I have so much potential, and I'll do anything to please him. Surely he sees that.

My phone rings, and Logan's sweet face pops up on the screen. I answer it happily, and my son chats with me about his day and the ice cream he's eaten.

When he's done, my mother gets on the line. "We need to talk," she tells me, her voice short. "If you're not taking him down there for school next year, you're going to have to sign over guardianship to me. You're not here, and I'll have to sign things."

"I'm not signing him over to you," I answer quickly.

"That's crazy. I can do all the school paperwork and send it to you."

"Ha! So you *aren't* planning on taking him," my mom says. It was a trap.

"That's not what I'm saying at all," I answer steadily. "I'm just saying if things don't work out and take longer than I anticipated, I don't need to sign over custody just for him to go to school there a little while longer."

"Why would it take longer?" my mother asks, and there's ice in her voice. I swear, I feel like she doesn't even like me anymore. "If it's a matter of money, I'll help. For Logan's sake."

Make sure to get that in there. Not for me, for Logan.

"It's not that," I answer. "Things just aren't settled here yet."

"With your married boyfriend?" she guesses, and correctly so. "I told you that wouldn't work out."

"You are wrong about him," I tell her, though I'm not so sure anymore.

She laughs. "I think that's what every mistress on earth must say."

"I'm more than a mistress, Mom," I argue.

She laughs again. "You're naïve," she decides. "I thought I raised you smarter than that."

"You raised me to hate men," I tell her. "Thank God I didn't do as you wanted. I'd be old and bitter, just like you."

"I have reasons to be bitter," she says, and then coughs. I wait, and her coughing fit lasts longer than I thought.

"Are you sick?" I ask. The cough is wet and raspy, and doesn't sound good.

"No. I'm fine. It's just a lingering cold."

"You should go to the doctor," I advise.

"I already did," she answers. "I'm fine."

But an idea has formed.

When we hang up, I look at Tessa's social media again. She's planning on going to some big black-tie event tonight with Ethan.

I text him.

I really need you.

He doesn't answer.

I really need you, I text again.

What's going on? he answers.

> *My aunt died. She was a second mom to me. I'm a wreck. Logan is there, arrangements have to be made, he will need to be brought here, my mom won't be in the right frame of mind to have him . . . I don't have the money . . .*

God, Linds, he answers. *I'm so sorry! That's terrible!*

Can you come over tonight? I really need you.

I'm supposed to be going to a huge thing with Tessa, he answers. *She'll kill me if I cancel now. It's in an hour. It's a big deal. Can I come over after?*

Please, babe, I answer. *I need you right now. I'm a mess.*

Okay, he answers simply.

While I wait, I watch Tessa's accounts. Sure enough, twenty minutes later, a new post goes up, Connor in a tux. "Plans have changed," she writes. "I'll be accompanied by this handsome fella tonight instead!"

Who says *fella*? I roll my eyes. She doesn't seem angry, and that's annoying.

When Ethan arrives, he hugs me immediately. He smells like cedar, like always, and I draw a long breath in.

"Are you okay?" he asks as he pulls away.

I nod my head. "I think I'm still in shock, actually." I manage a small smile, and he studies me.

"Can I get you anything?" he asks, even though we're in my apartment.

I shake my head. "Can you just sit with me?" I ask. He nods, and we sit on the couch. I tuck my feet up under me, and he puts his arm around my shoulders. I'm not sure if I'm imagining it, but he seems stiffer than normal.

"What happened?" he asks.

"Heart attack," I answer simply. "Logan and my mom were there. He's so upset."

"Of course he is. That's awful."

"I'm going to have to bring him here right away, after the funeral. My mom is with him now. I just don't know where I'll find the money. . . ."

Ethan pats my back awkwardly.

"It's okay. We'll figure something out," he finally says. I look up at him. Because this is a test. Is he willing to put everything aside to help me in my hour of need?

"We will?"

He pauses, then nods. "Yeah. Of course. I'll help you. I have to figure out how to do it without Tessa finding out because that's a huge chunk of money. But we'll figure it out."

"Where does she think you are right now?" I ask, my fingers curling around his.

"I told her someone on my crew had truck trouble and didn't have anyone else to call. It's a half-truth. You didn't have anyone else to call."

I snuggle into his side and pull his arm tighter around me.

"Thank you for coming. I don't know what I would've done if you hadn't. I don't know what I would do without you, Ethan. Do you promise me I won't ever have to be?"

He's quiet, and I'm still.

"Of course," he answers. But it took him a second, and I take a deep breath. I don't know what I've won, if anything at all. I had to lie to get Ethan here, so it doesn't really count.

It's time to press.

"Ethan, will you consider leaving Tessa for me?" I ask, my voice a whisper. "I need you. She doesn't. My entire life is falling apart, and you're the only real thing I have. You're everything to me. I need you."

His breath catches, and he's silent. I wait.

And wait.

"Please," I whisper again. "I need you."

"Okay," he finally answers. "I'll try to figure it out."

Victory exhales from my lips with my breath.

Finally.

thirty-one

TESSA

"I don't care what he said in that one moment. You are no competition for me," I spit.

She laughs. "You're right. We're in different age and weight brackets."

I want to kill her. I literally want to reach across the table and squeeze her neck until her eyes pop out. But I don't. She's no longer in handcuffs, and my son is resting nearby.

She stretches now, reaching for the ceiling.

"He might've told you he was leaving me," I say. "But you manipulated his emotions. And when it comes right down to it, he didn't leave me. Actions speak louder than words."

She opens her mouth to say something else, but Colt starts to thrash about. He throws off the blanket and moans, and I jump up and run to him. His eyes are open.

"Mom, I'm sorry I didn't tell you about Dad," he says, and he sounds anguished. "I'm sorry."

"It's okay, babe. It wasn't your story to tell," I assure him.

"Don't think about that now. You focus on getting better, okay?"

He nods, and his eyes seem to lose focus, then refocus. "Did Dad end it with her?"

"Yes, he did," I answer. "Don't fret, honey."

"I should kill him for that," he mutters, then rolls over, his eyes closing. I swallow hard and pull up the blanket. I hadn't wanted any of the kids to know. It's not a cross I want them to bear.

"I didn't want them to know," I tell Lindsey, when I return to the kitchen table.

"I didn't tell him on purpose," she defends herself.

"If you hadn't been in my house, he wouldn't have found out."

She can't argue with that.

"Are you going to tell Connor and Ava now?" she asks me as I stand up.

I scowl at her. "Of course not. Why should I? You're a thing of the past. They never need to know."

She looks stricken.

"Let me ask you something." I lean forward. "When I texted you, pretending to be Ethan, why did you answer? Why would you be willing to drive through a hurricane just to spend time with him?"

From across the table, she examines me, my face, my hands. She's carefully deciding what to say, I realize.

"Tessa . . ." She pauses for effect. "I knew it was you the entire time."

thirty-two

LINDSEY

I'm lying in bed, restless and alone.

After our conversation last night, Ethan hasn't said much to me. I try to watch TV, but nothing captures my interest. So I pick up my phone and break the rules. I text Ethan.

We decided months ago that I wouldn't text him after the workday ended, just in case Tessa saw his phone. We didn't want to take that chance, or at least, he didn't.

Tonight, I'm willing to risk it. Because he said he'd leave her. I take a picture of my bare breasts and send it along with: *Thinking about you.*

I put it aside, thinking he'll answer me tomorrow, but I'm surprised when he answers right away. He must be bored.

Nice headlights! he answers, and that feels weird because it's all he says. Normally he would be more engaged, more interested.

Good answer! I reply, lying. *Is Tessa not home?*

She's here.

Well, let me distract you. I take several more nude pics for him. I want him to be thinking about me tonight. Not her.

There's no answer.

Odd.

I wait.

There's still no answer.

Damn it. Why isn't he answering?

I pout in bed alone, flipping the TV back on. The laugh tracks start to annoy me, but I can't find anything better to watch. I check my phone. Nothing.

I doze off and on, and it's after midnight when my phone rings. It's odd to get a call this late, and I'm afraid something is wrong with Logan. I answer quickly.

"Hello?"

"Hey, it's me," Ethan says abruptly. "I've been thinking about things since last night, and when you asked me to leave Tessa, it took me by surprise. I'm sorry I said I'd think about it. Because I can't. This has to be over, Lindsey. I can't do this anymore."

My heart drops, thudding on the floor, and I can't swallow.

"Wait," I manage to say, but he interrupts.

"I'll help you get Logan here because I said I would," he says. "But that's it. This has to be done." Then he hangs up.

I sit up in bed, and I'm frozen in disbelief. That couldn't have just happened. He wouldn't do that.

He did not just break up with me.

How did we get HERE? I text him.

> *It's over, Lindsey. I know you were in my house. Colt told me. I've been struggling with this, and I know what I have to do. I have to end it.*

I pace the room. He chose her.

He chose her.

I sit on the couch and drink vodka straight from the bottle. It stings my lips, but I don't care. All of this work, and for what? *He chose her.*

It's a song that keeps playing, the words taunting me. He chose his wife.

Fuck.

I look around my apartment and try to focus on the good. But I wanted him. I invested in him. *I love him.*

It's a fact that I don't like. I didn't really mean to love him. It just happened. At first, it had been exciting, to take a man from his wife. I'd felt so powerful. It was a heady feeling. But then, I got to know him. He's funny and smart and handsome, and I'd fallen in love.

Now my heart hurts.

I cry and drink, cry and drink. I check my phone, looking at her social media, hoping for news. If Colt told Ethan about me being at the house, maybe he'd told his mom, too. But there's nothing. Of course not. She wouldn't air this to the public. It would be far too embarrassing.

Around 1:00 a.m., I get a Gmail notification, and my heart lurches when I see his name. *Ethan Taylor.* I click on it.

Linds,

I'm sorry I was so abrupt on the phone. I didn't mean to be. I hate that I have to do this, but I hope you don't hate me.

E

I'm limp as I read his words. He's really leaving me. He chose her. I cry until I fall asleep.

When I wake, sunlight streams into my living room, and my head is pounding.

It takes me a minute to remember what had happened.

Ethan has broken it off. He's chosen Tessa. It can't be real. I'm younger, prettier, more understanding. I am so perfect for him. I made myself perfect.

My phone is still in my hand, my email pulled up. There's another one from him, and my heart hurts as I read it.

Linds,

I'm sorry if I've hurt you. You didn't deserve this. I know you came into this relationship with your eyes open, knowing that I was (and am) married. But I still want you to know that I would never purposely hurt you like this. I made a mistake. I made a lot of mistakes. But hurting you is the one I regret the most.

Forgive me,
E

Tears drip onto my phone screen. He loved me. He still loves me. I feel it.

I am utterly broken. I call in sick to work and curl up on the couch. Every single cell in me is sad. I'm floating on a sea of pain. I swig at the vodka to kill the pain, even though it's only seven in the morning.

I'm eating ice cream for breakfast when my phone rings. Ethan. I scramble for it. But it's not Ethan. It's Logan.

"Mommy, I miss you," he says, and his voice is small and sweet. It melts my heart, and I know I'd do anything for him.

Just like Ethan would do anything for Colt. Colt must've asked him to do this.

I chat with my son for a few minutes, and when I hang up, I know for certain, deep in my heart, that his children and their loyalty to Tessa are the only reasons Ethan would break up with me.

I think of Tessa, her smug face, and her stupid, successful life. She doesn't deserve any of it. She doesn't deserve Ethan.

It's her fault Ethan had to end it. It's all her fault.

I realize, in a sudden surge of startling clarity, what I need to do. An idea settles around me, fluttering and dark, like a cape I draw closely around my shoulders. She needs to pay for destroying what was mine.

I rage all day long, pacing my apartment like a woman gone wild. I pull at my hair. I vomit in the toilet. I stalk Tessa online. I call her phone. She never answers. Ethan doesn't either.

It's over, and I'm alone.

I don't remember the last time I felt this way, so bereft, so broken, such a failure. Causing a man to stray is the easiest thing in the world. But keeping him is a different story, I realize. Keeping him is the hard part.

There has to be something I can do. There just has to be.

I grab my keys and jump in the car, headed to Ethan's job site. His truck isn't there. Fuck.

I drive out to their house, taking the curves way too fast. I park down the road and hike to the beach, then peer through the trees.

Ethan's truck is outside and so is Tessa's car.

I reach for the binoculars. Indoors, Ethan and Tessa are sitting at the table. It looks like they might be arguing, though I can't really tell. He tries to put his hand on her shoulder, but she yanks away. She shakes her head, moving farther away. I wonder what they're fighting about. Is it me? I hate that he's trying so hard. She doesn't deserve him. I do.

I pull out the notebook from my bag.

Ethan,

I love you so much. I can be anything you need me to be. I only need you. No baggage, no complaints. I want you. I want all of you. Your scars, your bad jokes, your beautiful face. I accept you as you are. No matter what mistakes you make. My love for you is unconditional.

Please give me another chance. Don't end this. It's too good.

I don't want to live without you. I don't know if I can.

Love always,
Linds

I look through the binoculars again. They're still there, arguing now. Tessa's arms are going this way and that as she gestures. Ethan sits, listening, taking everything she has to say, like a whipped dog. It makes me shudder. I would never make him feel like that. I would never emasculate him.

Quickly, I skid down the hill and through the trees to their driveway. I sprint to the side of his truck, folding my note beneath his wiper blade. Then I sprint back to my spot and look again.

They're still there. They haven't noticed me.

Good.

He just needs to know that I'm willing to change, to never push, to never question; that I'll be anything he wants me to be in exchange for even a little bit of the stability that Tessa has.

She never goes to bed wondering if he will still be in her life when she wakes up, and I deserve that, too. She has everything, and I'm only asking for a little of it. If he answers my note, if he gives me another chance, I'll change. I'd do anything for that kind of stability.

I'm so sad, so tired, that I don't notice my legs growing heavy, my arms falling asleep. I wait and wait, until dusk comes. I'm actually growing sleepy when their front door opens and Ethan comes out.

He approaches his truck, and his hand is on the door handle. He opens it and climbs inside, the big engine roaring to life.

My heart sinks. He didn't see the note. Fuck.

He backs out and noses down the driveway. Then he stops. He gets out and grabs the note.

My breath catches in my throat as I watch him read it in the cab of the truck.

Then he continues down the road.

I wait, but he doesn't call. I stand there limply, my heart filling with lead as I realize he's not going to. He probably crumpled it up and threw it out the window. A lump forms in my throat, and I can't swallow it.

Ten minutes pass, and Tessa disappears from sight. She's probably crying in her bed like the pathetic heap she is. I wait to see if she'll come back, but she doesn't. And Ethan doesn't either.

Numbly, I walk down the beach. My feet feel like concrete blocks, my legs like matchsticks.

I wonder if Ethan saw my car as he drove past. I check the front window, but there's not a note.

I'm empty as I drive home. I can't even cry. He really doesn't want me, and I can't believe it. My heart wants to stop beating. I don't want to breathe. I don't want to feel.

I go outside and stand near the pond. Is it possible to drown yourself? I should know this, but I can't seem to think straight.

I'm still pondering that when my phone vibrates. I pull it out and find texts from a strange number. My heart stops as I read the words.

I hope you don't hate me.

Don't hurt yourself.

This is a new number. No one knows about it.

My mouth opens, then closes.

He thought I meant I would kill myself if we didn't get back together? I'm startled, but then it doesn't matter. A smile forms, brighter than the sun and as wide as the ocean.

He wants me.

He wants me.

He wants me.

thirty-three

TESSA

Ethan bought a burner phone and texted Lindsey with it. It can't be. *It can't.*

Did he really break things off, then get back together with her? It wasn't until this moment that I believed it was possible he could actually have feelings for her.

The entire world slams into me, the weight of it, the breadth of it, the sounds. Everything at once, and I faint.

The next thing I know, I'm sprawled on the kitchen floor, and Lindsey is next to me on her knees.

"Get off me!" I snap, shoving her hands away. My temple throbs from where I hit the stone. I rub at it. I feel sick. I contemplate vomiting but fight back the urge. I won't let her see the effect this has on me. I swallow hard. "So explain the texts I saw on his iPad if he uses a burner phone instead."

"We rarely use his regular phone," she says, rocked back now and looking at me. "I texted myself from Ethan's phone and then deleted the messages so he wouldn't see. I was hoping you'd see it on his laptop or something. I was sick of waiting for him to tell you. When that text came in yesterday, I knew immediately it was from you."

The room seems to spin. Ethan went back to her.

"But why would you . . . why would you want to continue with a man who wouldn't leave his wife?"

"He didn't want to be with you anymore," she tells me. "But he wanted to wait to leave for a while because of the kids. They're unsettled because of Colt. He wanted to wait until they were on more stable footing. Because he's a good father. I'm not a fling, Tessa."

Colors blend into sounds as I listen to her words. Is she telling the truth?

Thunder cracks, ripping apart the night, and I startle, sucking a breath in. The storm still rages outside, but the one in my heart is bigger. The one in my heart might tear me apart. This night is a nightmare. My life is a nightmare.

Colt moans again, and I woodenly cross to the living room, kneeling before him. He's fine, muttering in his sleep. I pull the blanket up again, even though I know he'll kick it back off. I can't feel my fingers. I can't feel my toes. I can't feel my heart.

I'm in shock. Everything should hurt, but it doesn't. I can't feel a thing.

"You know you'll never get a cent of my money," I tell Lindsey. "I made it. It's mine."

She shakes her head. "I don't care about that. Ethan makes his own."

Everything I've lived this entire year has been a lie. Every conversation with Ethan. Every time he's said he loves me. All lies.

246

I can't seem to breathe as I return to the kitchen and lean against the sink. My life has changed in a heartbeat and all because of this woman. A fling I could possibly get past. But this . . .

If this is all true. If it's not, she's a sick, perverted sociopath.

Either way, rage envelopes me, suddenly and completely. The heat fills me up, burning me, and my vision is all red, bright red. My vision is blood.

I charge into her, knocking her chair over, and I can't tell if the loud crack I hear is the chair or her skull hitting the stone floor. She wrenches away, rolling over, her bony ass in the air. She staggers to her feet and leans against the wall.

"I take it you believe me, then?" she asks, unflappable, as though there wasn't a rivulet of blood trickling down her cheekbone.

"No," I tell her, even though it's a lie. I think it's a lie. Is it a lie? "You're just a stupid cunt who can't support herself, who is desperately trying to get a man. If I let you turn me against him, then you've won."

"I've already won." She laughs. She's sprawled against the wall, her face bleeding. I'm holding myself up against the sink. My wedding ring is spun around on my finger, the diamond cutting into my palm. I twist it back around, and the metal feels like a lie.

"He gave me jewelry, too," she says, watching my fingers move. She fiddles with a silver pendant, a tiny aquamarine.

"But not a wedding ring," I tell her, because that's the one thing I know will hurt.

She blinks slowly. I smile and straighten my ring like a crown. *I* am Queen. I splay my hand on my hip, aiming it directly at her.

Her face is a frozen mask, and my heart is a block of ice. We are at a stalemate, with nowhere to go.

Between us, her phone is on the table. And suddenly . . . suddenly . . . it lights up, illuminating the dark kitchen, as text after text rolls in.

"We have a signal," Lindsey breathes. She snatches her phone and looks at it. She doesn't bother to read the texts; instead, she punches a few keys, then turns it to me, holding it out like an offering.

She has it pulled up to a contact. Ethan. My chest constricts.

"Go ahead," she urges me. "Call. See who answers."

I can't. I can't. I can't. I need to call an ambulance for Colt.

And yet, I need to know.

It will only take a second.

I step to her, without feeling my feet, and take the phone. It's cold, foreign in my hand. I put it on speaker, and I push Call. Lindsey is smug.

One ring.

Two rings.

Three.

Then a man's voice.

"Hello?"

It's Ethan.

thirty-four

LINDSEY

E than can only come to see me in short spurts and moments. Stolen minutes, carefully guarded from Tessa.

"It's just for a while," he promises me, after a quickie in a parking lot. "Just a while longer."

I make a little home for him in my apartment. It's our little nest, his respite from the world and Tessa's nagging. She is driving him away. He is a good man. She made him this way.

"When you leave her, you can come here," I tell him comfortingly. "Until we can find a bigger place. We'll need something where the kids have their own rooms."

He's so tired from juggling everything. Yet I know I'm important to him or he wouldn't bother trying. He wants me. He needs me. He'll do anything to keep me.

Days pass, then a couple of weeks. I start to push Ethan a bit more.

"Colt is still in a bad way," he tells me every time. "He's

unstable. The kids are both in therapy about it. I can't leave now. What kind of father would that make me?"

At the cost of his fatherhood, I steal from my motherhood. I put off bringing Logan here, and it broke his heart. I tell myself it's for the best, that his life will be a hundred times better when Ethan and I are together. But his tears break my heart, and they are hard to forget.

Logan has begun to doubt me, and I myself start to question my strength. What if Ethan never thinks it's a good time? What will I do then?

My mother lectures me constantly, berating me, shaming me. I know I deserve it, but it still pisses me off. She has no right. She doesn't know what I'm doing to ensure Logan has a good life. She'll see someday. But for now, she's just being a bitch. She's just like Tessa.

One day, I follow her to her salon. When she's inside, I call to see if Julie happens to be free for an emergency cut, and God is on my side, because she has an opening after she finishes Tessa's color. I smile, pull my car next to Tessa's, and calmly, over and over, I slam my car door into hers, until hers has a scraped-up dent in the red paint.

Her stylist never knows who I really am or what I've done. I feel smug when Julie greets me with a hug, beautifying me and strengthening the tools in my arsenal.

"You just missed Tessa," she tells me with a grin.

I grin back. I know. I planned it that way . . . two ships passing in the night.

Ethan comes to me that night, complaining that Tessa is so careless that she's dented her car. I smile and soothe him, never saying a word, but I make a mental note to fix my car door before he sees it.

Someday soon, *everyone* will know that I am important enough for Ethan to choose me over her. I'm his safe place, his respite. I ease his suffering. I am his soft place to land.

"Tessa doesn't trust me," he tells me after a particularly rough lovemaking session later that night. I stay understanding, accepting whatever he wants to give me. I know he's just taking out his frustrations with Tessa. It's not me he resents. It's her. "I think she suspects something."

I look at him in the moonlight pouring in from the window. In this moment, I can see that he's changed. He's different from the man I fell in love with. *Of course he is,* I tell myself. She's ruined him. Her bitterness would wear on anyone. He'll change back when it's all over, when he's fully mine.

He starts to become more and more careful, convinced that his wife knows. He starts canceling dates. He starts saying yes to more trips and not taking me.

It hurts, and it makes me seethe that she has that kind of power. But then . . . something amazing happens. Ethan texts me from his burner phone and tells me that he's been delayed in New York.

And then . . . then a text comes in from his regular phone number.

> *Hey babe. I got home early, and I'm at home alone.*
> *Wanna come ride out the storm with me?* ☺

Sometimes fate just needs a little push.

thirty-five

TESSA

The phone shakes in my palm as my husband answers his mistress.

"Hello?" Ethan says again, and he sounds a little annoyed. "Linds? You can't call me for a while. Until I work things out with Tessa. You know she knows." At his words, both my head and Lindsey's jerk to attention.

Lindsey's horror is equal to my own. We share the same expression, and our hearts both pound.

"Ethan," Lindsey says slowly. "I thought you were going to leave Tessa."

There's silence on the other end.

"Ethan, where are you?" she asks.

"At the airport. Waiting for the first available flight so I can fly home and fix this mess. What do you need?"

Lindsey's eyes meet mine, and we're both in shock. He sounds so cold to her. Her eyes say a million things. . . . *He can't. He didn't. He wouldn't betray me.*

Mine say only one. *He would*.

"What do you need?" Ethan asks again, and he's perfunctory. Lindsey opens her mouth, trying to decide what to say. "Listen, I've gotta go. I'll call you later," my husband says and hangs up.

My blood is ice, freezing up my veins. Why is he even still talking to her?

Lindsey and I are left staring at each other. I'm limp. She's devastated.

I don't know what to say. Neither does she.

"Listen," I tell her, figuring now is as good a time as any. "I found something earlier. After you told me about All the Fish. I logged in, and I found the messages you said I would find. But I also found more. Another woman."

"I can't believe it," she says, and she strums the table with her skinny fingers. I spin my ring around my finger, a nervous habit. With each rotation, the diamond catches my flesh. "I can't believe it."

"Can't you?" I finally manage. "He's a cheater. Did you think you would change him?"

Lindsey stares at me, and I exhale. She sucks in a ragged breath. *Why do I feel sorry for her? Am I insane?*

Everything in my life is a lie. Except for my kids. Wordlessly, I get up and check on Colton. He's quiet now, though his forehead is still sweaty. I stroke his hair away from his face, and Lindsey watches me, still reeling from Ethan's betrayal. It's new to her, this feeling. I know what it's like.

"You're a good mother," she says, her voice cool and detached. "I guess you always knew what was important, after all."

"Marriages are important, too," I answer. "Just as important.

But only if both people are committed. I guess I was deluding myself there."

"Maybe he just got a taste of the excitement that cheating brings," Lindsey ponders, trying to figure it out, make sense of it. I get it. I did the same thing. "Maybe he got addicted to that."

"Maybe. Or maybe he's just a selfish asshole," I suggest. I hold Colt's hand, allowing the weight of it to ground me.

"That's not the Ethan I know," she says, defending him.

I lift an eyebrow. "Isn't it? You knew all along he was willing to treat *me* in such a way. You're only just now seeing it directed at *you.*"

She thinks on that, and her shoulders slump.

"God," she mutters. "I'm so stupid."

"I know just how you feel."

"At least you didn't . . . haven't . . . compromised yourself," she says, a little wounded bird. "I've done terrible things. I've disappointed my son. He probably thinks he's not important to me."

She looks away, out the window, at the rain.

"Then you should fix that," I suggest. "He's more important than Ethan ever was. He's your child. He loves you unconditionally. You should return the favor."

"I do," she says defensively. "I just can't survive on my own."

"You sell yourself short," I tell her, staring at my son's sleeping face. It's gaunt and hollow, and he's oblivious to the storm surrounding him . . . both the one in the house and the one outside. "You can do anything you set your mind to."

"Why are you being nice to me?" she asks. "I've been horrible to you."

I lift my gaze to the girl in the kitchen. And she *is* a girl.

An inexperienced, immature girl who got in over her head and believed the same lies I had.

"We were both betrayed," I tell her. "And I've been horrible to you, too."

"Maybe he'll change."

I laugh because I can see she really believes that. Just like I had this morning.

"Fool me once, shame on you. Fool me twice, shame on me," is all I say.

Lindsey lowers her head to the table and cries. I try not to listen, but her shoulders shake as she wails for everything she believes she has lost. Everything that was mine in the first place, everything that was never hers, but also maybe was never even mine.

I release Colt's hand, placing it carefully next to his hip and get up. I walk straight to the side bar in the dining room. It's dark in here, with only the light of the candles, but I know exactly where everything is. I reach for the Glenlivet, Ethan's favorite. I carry it and two whiskey glasses to the table and set them down with a *thunk*. Lindsey doesn't look up. She's still sniffling, and her shoulders are quaking.

I have no sympathy, for her or for me. We're both stupid. I pour two glasses and shove one toward her.

"Drink."

She looks up, watery-eyed, and peers at the glass. She starts to shake her head, but I push the glass again.

"Bottoms up," I tell her. "You'll feel better after."

I do as I say and gulp it all in one fell swoop. It burns like fire going down, but my chest warms up nicely.

My phone rings. I see it light up on the countertop, but I

don't make a move to answer it. Instead, I watch Lindsey as she shoots the whiskey. She shudders and rushes for water. I laugh mirthlessly. What a child.

I'd been the same once. That was back before Ethan had jaded me. Broken me. That was before her.

As Lindsey cracks open a bottle of water and guzzles it, I think about my life. About how much of it I've wasted on Ethan.

"I'm forty years old," I say out loud. "I've been with him for over twenty years. Now I don't know if he's ever been faithful to me."

I think about all his late nights, the excuses I had bought. I had trusted him without question. In fact, I went so far as to tell my friends, *Ethan might be many things, but he's as loyal as the day is long.*

That cracks me up now, a wretched burst of hysterical laughter that startles Lindsey. She watches me cautiously.

"I've got to pick up the pieces," I say, the laughter subsiding.

"Me, too," she says in her little girl voice, with her little girl mouth. You couldn't pay me enough to be in her shoes. At least I have money. At least I can rebuild myself, my life, in comfort.

My heart is broken, but it will heal. Someday. Maybe.

"I wonder who the other girls are," Lindsey says, pacing again, her energy frenetic. She's worried now, fretting about her competition. She still doesn't get it.

"It doesn't matter," I tell her.

"Maybe he's a sociopath or something," Lindsey wonders. "He needs therapy."

I shrug. "It doesn't matter to me. Not anymore."

I pick up the phone to call 911. "Hello. My son is a hemophiliac with a leg wound. I administered clotting factor, and he seems to be stable. But he needs to get to a hospital. There's a broken piece of wood in his wound, and we're afraid to move it. We only just now got a cell signal. I live out on Yaggy Lane," I tell them. "A tree came down in the storm. It's blocking the road, and we can't get out."

The dispatcher asks me for details, and I go back to Colton. I check his pulse as she asks.

"It's better than it was," I tell her. "It's ninety-nine now. It was probably a hundred and fifty before."

"Will he respond to you?"

I shake him gently. "Colt."

He opens his eyes. "Yeah?" He's bleary-eyed and out of it, but he answers.

"Yes," I tell her.

"The storm has caused extensive damage in your area," the dispatcher tells me. "Your son sounds stable. Keep a close eye on him, and we'll get someone out to you as soon as we can. Please be advised that it might be closer to morning. We'll do what we can. Should his condition change, if he has trouble breathing or stops responding, call us back right away. Also, do not move that piece of wood. The doctors need to do it in case it is staunching the bleeding. If it is, he could bleed to death if you try."

Fuck. Lindsey truly saved his life.

"Okay." I hang up. I turn to Lindsey. I want to tell her thank you again, but I don't. "It could be morning by the time they get here. Who knows."

She rests her head on the table again.

"So," I stare at her, crossing my arms in front of me. "You knew it was me contacting you pretending to be Ethan."

She nods, and her eyes are puffy from crying.

"Yes."

"Why did you play along?"

"I thought I knew what you were doing. I thought you wanted to catch Ethan in the act, and that was in my best interest. I had no idea that *this*"—she gestures around my house with her hand—"was what you were planning."

"But you came here. Did you know he wasn't here?"

"He'd just texted me on the burner phone and said he was in New York."

"So why did you put the handcuffs on?"

She looks at me. "Because I had no idea you were such a crazy bitch! I thought you were trying to trap Ethan. I didn't know—I *could never have known*—that you had this planned. God. I thought you were just setting me up for Ethan, for a confrontation, to blow things out of the water. I had no idea that you'd lost your shit."

Her naïveté shows again, and once more, my guilt swells. She had no clue. She had no idea what she was dealing with or how far over her head she was.

"You shouldn't trust people," I caution her. "There are crazies out there."

"I know that now." She looks down her nose at me, and I almost laugh.

"Besides," she continues, in a steely tone, "I'm not a child. I had a backup plan."

"A backup plan?" I arch an eyebrow at the child in front of me. She stretches as though she's bored, and nods.

"Yeah. Hang on."

She walks through the kitchen, past my son on the couch,

and into my bedroom. While she's gone, I look at my phone. Ethan texted.

I need to talk to you.

I decide not to answer it. Not yet. I don't know what I'm going to do about him. Right now, the mere sight of his name makes me see red.

I hear Lindsey coming back, and I put my phone down. She stands in the doorway, a gun in her hand.

"See?" She smiles. "A backup plan."

thirty-six

TESSA

I eye the gleaming gun. The barrel almost looks blue in the candlelight.

"Is that Ethan's?" I ask her, trying to stay calm. Lindsey nods.

"Very good."

"I bought that for his birthday last year," I tell her conversationally, my words slow and even.

It's in her hand, and her hand is at her side, but the second I move to stand up, she lifts it.

"Ethan taught me to use this," she says matter-of-factly. "So that I could defend myself."

"Why? Do you have a stalker?" I ask, my mouth dry. "I do." She rolls her eyes.

"Ethan may have fucked me over," she tells me, and her eyes are red, "but you fucked me over, too. I would've known he was slipping away."

"So Ethan cheating on you, *and cheating on me*, with other

women is my fault?" I level a gaze at her and hope she realizes how ridiculous she sounds. But she only nods.

"I would've noticed had I not been so preoccupied with you."

"What difference does it make now?" I ask tightly. "He's gone. And here you and I sit at odds with each other. We should be focused on him."

"I can't. I'm too pissed at him."

"Me, too," I agree. "The pain makes it hard to focus, doesn't it? But think of this: You've spent the better part of a year on him. I've spent over twenty years. Twenty. Years. That's almost as long as you've been *alive.*"

Jesus. She's a child. She's just a kid, like Ava or Connor or Colt. She didn't have the capacity to know what she was stepping into, nor does she have the capacity to handle it now.

I wanted her to feel my pain.

And now she does.

Her eyes are glossed over with it.

She doesn't react. I examine her. Her eyes are glassy, almost wild again, like they were earlier. Her hand shakes, and her feet are bare. I'm penned in the kitchen. I can't run. Colt's on the couch. I'd never leave him.

I can try to overpower her, which could wind up with one of us dead, or I can try to talk sense into her.

"Don't bother," she tells me. "I don't want to hear it."

"But what's your endgame?" I ask her. "Are you going to shoot me? And say what? It was self-defense? Are you going to shoot Colt, too?"

Her expression wavers now, and she glances toward the living room.

"He hasn't done anything to you," I say quietly. "All he's done is exist."

"I'm not going to shoot Colt," she snaps back. "He's not even awake. But I could say that you tried to kill me, and I shot you in self-defense."

"You're wearing my clothing, Lindsey," I remind her. "That would make for an interesting sequence of events in your story."

Her nostrils flare as she thinks.

"Where was your gun this whole time, Lindsey?" I ask, hoping to get her talking about anything other than killing me. My heart is surprisingly calm.

"It was in the side of my purse. The outside pocket. You're so stupid that when you were going through it, you didn't even notice."

How did I not notice a gun? Good lord.

A tear streaks down her face, then another. Her hands shake and shake, and I see that the emotional impact of finding out about Ethan has put her in shock. It's rendered her illogical. Just like me when I found out about her. Oh, the irony.

"I can't believe he'd do this to me," she says yet again. She's a child who believed the best of someone, even after seeing his worst.

I sigh. "You're worth more than him," I tell her. "I've been trying to tell you that all along. You're pretty and smart. You deserve someone who makes you his entire world . . . someone who doesn't give you his leftover time."

"Don't act like you care," she snaps at me, and the tears are running now, flowing onto her shirt. She glances back over at Colt and listens to his deep breathing, his quiet snorts.

"Your son causes you so much worry, and yet you still love him."

"Of course I do," I say. "He's my son. His illness is not his fault."

"You must love him unconditionally," she says, and she sounds bitter now, far from the gullible child she was a moment ago. "I didn't do a single thing to my father, and he left me anyway."

Realization slams into me. I'd been right all along about her daddy issues. She feels unworthy. She slides the gun up to her neck, poking it at the hollow where her jaw meets her ear. She scratches her skin with it, then holds it there.

It's aimed at her head. I breathe in pants. I don't know what to do. Is she going to kill herself in my kitchen? I don't want to see that.

And I don't want it to happen.

"That was your father's loss," I tell her. "He didn't realize what he was missing. He was being selfish. It wasn't your fault."

She looks at me with haunted eyes. "I wasn't good enough for him," she says bluntly. "And I've never been good enough for anyone. Not enough for them to stay. Look at Ethan. I did everything right. I was everything he could possibly want me to be. And I wasn't enough."

"I think there was a lot more going on in his head than either of us was privy to," I say.

"You don't know what it's like to be me," she says yet again. "I'm not even good enough to raise my own kid." She laughs, a hollow sound. "At least he has my mother. I've never been good to him. All I do is cause disappointment."

I'm frozen with the irony that I'm pleading with my husband's mistress not to kill herself. It's an odd thing, but when a person is faced with the true balance of life and death, it's a weighty, weighty thing. It's something I don't want to witness. It's something I feel a responsibility to prevent.

She is a life, and all lives are valuable, aren't they?

"Lindsey," I say now. "You're the only one who can be Logan's mother. Only you can love him the way a mother does. No one else can replace that. Not even a grandmother."

She looks at me cautiously. "Do you really think that?"

I nod. "I know that," I tell her. "I'm a mother, too. I know. And I'm a daughter. When something is really wrong, all I want to do is call my mom. And look at Colt," I point out. "When he feels too unsafe, he comes home. *To me.* That's what mothers do for their children. That's what they are."

She thinks on that and wipes away the tears on her cheeks. "But I'm not like you."

I shake my head. "No, you're not. Because you're you. But you can walk out of this house and fly straight to Arizona, and you can start over if you want. You can rebuild things and never look back. Ethan is toxic. Your son, though, Logan, is pure love."

Her eyes close, and her lashes flutter against her cheek.

I suck in a breath.

The gun dangles from loose fingertips.

Then it clatters onto the stone.

I exhale.

I take a few steps, and before I know it, before I plan it, I'm standing in front of her, and I pull her to me. I hug her, and she lets me. She's limp and alone, and I'm all she has in this moment.

I'm a woman embracing her husband's mistress.

thirty-seven

TESSA

Lindsey cries for an hour, slumped into the window seat, listening to the passing storm. She's desolate, inconsolable. Finally, she sits straight up.

"I'm going to call Ethan."

I lift an eyebrow. "Why bother? He's just going to lie."

"I still have to know what he has to say for himself. Besides, he didn't just cheat on you or me; he cheated on these kids."

I shake my head. She wasn't thinking of my kids when *she* was screwing him, but that doesn't matter now.

She dials the phone. It rings and rings, and just when I think he won't answer because it's 4:00 a.m., he does. She puts him on speaker, and I can tell he'd been asleep.

"Lindsey?" he asks thickly. "What's wrong?"

"You're a cheating asshole," she snaps. "That's what's wrong."

He tries to deny it, as I knew he would, but unlike me when I found out, Lindsey all-out rails.

I had cried. I'd sat like a stone, trying to comprehend. I was stunned into silence. I was hurt. I was angry. I was confused. I was crazed. But I still held myself somewhat in check with him, like a piece of me was still clinging to vestiges of our past.

But not Lindsey. She doesn't have a past like ours to cling to.

She rages like the storm, like it gave her its destructive energy as it died outside, and she channeled it in here. She rages with the energy of the young, not caring if it will change anything, not fearing the loss of the fuel she expends upon it. She calls him everything she can think of, spewing every hateful thing imaginable.

"You're a selfish prick," she finally tells him, winding down, venomous and hateful. He tries to offer her excuses, to lie, but she won't have it. "You're a liar," she says bluntly. "You don't even know how to tell the truth."

"Listen," he tries to say. "I was just aimlessly chatting with that woman. I forgot to disable my account, and I got notifications when I got new messages. It stroked my ego. That's all."

"Were you ever going to leave Tessa?" she spits. My heart stops.

"Probably not," he admits, much to my surprise. "But that doesn't mean I don't love you. I do. That girl . . . I was just chatting. She's nothing."

My gut constricts. That's exactly what he'd told me about her. Hearing these words now, coming out of his own mouth, are daggers to my heart. Lindsey hadn't lied. He'd told her he was leaving. He'd been having his cake and eating it, too. We were both fools.

"So, Ethan," I break in now, since he's on speakerphone and I can't contain it any longer. "Exactly when were you planning on telling me that you love someone else?"

There is dead silence on the other end, and then I hear him breathe.

"Tess?" he utters, in disbelief, in terror.

"Oh yes, my love," I say sweetly. "Your girlfriend and I have been catching up tonight. It seems there's a lot we didn't know."

"Tessa, please," he begs me now. "It's not what it seems. I couldn't break it off with her because she was suicidal. She threatened to kill herself if I did."

I glance at her, but she shakes her head fiercely. "That's not true. The only time I ever wanted to die was tonight, when I found out you'd been lying to me all along, Ethan. Because I exchanged being a good mother with waiting for you, and it was the stupidest thing I ever did."

Ethan doesn't even ask about the mother comment. I don't give him a chance.

"You've been lying to me, too, Ethan," I tell him, and now he's a cornered dog. "And it's over."

"No, it's not," he argues. "I'll be on the next plane. I'll be there in two hours. We'll talk about this. You'll see . . . I had no choice. She was emotionally holding me hostage. I got in over my head. None of this was supposed to happen."

"You're such a prick," I tell him. "You made the conscious choice to lie to me. If any of this shit was even close to the truth, you would've told me. But you didn't. Because you wanted to keep getting your dick wet in two different women, and maybe even more. Fuck you. We're done."

I hang up.

It's abrupt, startling, final. We're no longer Ethan and Tessa. In this moment, I'm just Tessa. Maybe I have been for a long, long time and just didn't know it.

Ethan tries to call my phone immediately, but I let it go to voicemail and put it on speaker.

"Tess, please. I've really fucked up. I got myself into something that just spiraled, and I got out of control. But I'll do anything to keep you. You can play this aloud right now for Lindsey to hear. Lindsey, it's over. It's over with everyone but you, Tess. I love you. I'll be home in a couple of hours. Please, just wait for me. Talk to me."

Lindsey and I stare at each other, and our hearts both break at once.

I see her swallow.

"You were fierce," I tell her. "You had the ability to speak the truth to him. I was too shell-shocked. I was too careful about calling names and not wanting to say things I couldn't take back . . . out of habit, I guess. You, though . . . you didn't hold back."

She shakes her head. "I have the advantage of knowing the whole story. You didn't."

That's true. I saw what Ethan wanted me to see. The Ethan he portrayed to the world. I'm still having a hard time reconciling that with the man I just hung up on.

"I feel so stupid," I say, sitting down next to her in the window seat. Together, we listen to the rain that has died down to a light spattering. "I can't believe I trusted him."

"You thought you could," she says simply. "You were supposed to be able to."

Neither of us cry. I think we've both run out of tears.

"There's something I learned a long time ago from my granddad," I tell her. I feel the warmth from her shoulder leaning into mine, and all I can think of is how my husband has damaged this girl, how he's reduced her to thinking she's nothing, how he's diminished her.

I reach over and take her hand. She lets me. Her fingernails are jagged and broken from our struggles in the bedroom. They seem a lifetime ago now.

"My granddad taught me that people will always treat you how you allow them to treat you," I say softly.

I look her in the eye, and she nods. "Okay."

"I mean it," I tell her. "We've allowed Ethan to treat us this way because we believed him. Now that we know the truth, we pick up the pieces and we repair what he broke. Not in him, because we can't do that. *In us.* That's what we can do."

I feel her pain. I sense it as she breathes it out, in this room where Ethan sat and conversed with yet another woman while I was sleeping peacefully in our bed and while Lindsey was waiting for him in her apartment. I feel her sadness, and I feel her devastation. Earlier tonight, I would've rejoiced in it. I would've said she deserved all of it, and more. But everything feels different now. *I'm* different.

thirty-eight

LINDSEY

I go through my phone, and one by one, I delete all of Ethan's messages. Every single text, every single email. With each one, I feel lighter and lighter.

I watch Tessa go through his computer. I don't ask what she finds, but I do watch her face. Her lips get tight, her face pinched. Each time, I know she's found more women he was flirting with.

"In the vein of honesty," I tell her, "I did set out to get him."

"But he contacted you first." She looks up from the desk. "He was on a dating site."

"Yeah, but I don't really think he intended to meet someone. He was testing the waters. He felt alone, and he just wanted someone to talk to."

"I can't believe you're still defending him," Tessa says, shaking her head. "You've got to stop being so naïve."

"I'm not being naïve," I answer, and I think of Ethan's face, the way he laughed, the way he cocked his head. "He's a good person, deep down. I believe that. He got caught up in the excitement of it all. And I did manipulate him."

Tessa sighs, then lays her head down while still looking at me.

"Yes, you did. But he's a grown man, and as such, he should've just come to me and told me that he was hurting, that he felt alone."

"I think this is a midlife crisis," I offer, and Tessa starts to laugh.

"What would you know about a midlife anything?"

I laugh, too, and shrug. "I've read about them."

"Well, most men don't go out and get a mistress," Tessa snaps. "Maybe go out and buy a Corvette, join a gym, or something."

"I'm not trying to excuse him," I tell her. I don't even know what I'm trying to do, but I do feel responsible. "All I'm saying is that people make mistakes. This didn't happen overnight. Maybe he really did get sucked into the excitement of it all, and things got out of control. Maybe you could work it out if he's willing to work on his issues."

"I wouldn't even know where to begin on his issues," Tessa says, closing her eyes wearily. "I wasn't aware that he had any."

"Look, all I know is that when he talked about you, he was bothered." It pains me now to tell her, but I've got to stop lying. "He was a man who loved his wife. I can't deny that."

"Why are you saying this?" She opens her eyes and looks at me again. "Why do you care?"

"I think we share some things now," I say simply. "I don't know. It's a mess, and I'm part of it. And I hate that your kids will be hurt."

"Well, that ship has sailed. Colt already knows. I can't believe he didn't tell me."

"He probably thought Ethan should be the one to tell you. Or maybe he was hoping you'd never have to find out. Or maybe he didn't want to face it himself. Kids don't like thinking that their parents are human."

"Just like your mother is human," she says. "I know you're angry with her. For things that you think she did wrong when you were growing up and maybe even for the way she treats you now. But as a mother, I can tell you, sometimes the things I want to say come out wrong."

"Now you're defending my mother?"

"Well, in the vein of honesty." She shrugs. "I've got nothing left to lose. I've lost so much tonight already."

"So you were just driving home from your parents', and this all slapped you across the face? You honestly had no suspicions at all? Ethan thought you were starting to guess."

Tessa shakes her head. "Not at all. I had no clue. Looking back now, I should've. But I didn't know I was supposed to be looking for this."

I look away, at the richly paneled walls and expensive artwork. This room feels like Ethan, and it hurts to be in here, among his things, among his life. It's odd. Just months ago, I loved sneaking around here, being a part of things without anyone knowing. Now, I can't wait to leave.

"Well, if anything, I think this will help me grow, you know, into a better person and all that," I say aloud.

"That's the mark of maturity," Tessa answers. "Take a bad situation and learn from it. Grow from it. I know I'm going to."

"Are you going to leave him?" I'm afraid to ask, afraid of the answer. I know I shouldn't care, because I'm not going to be in this picture, no matter what. But I still want to know.

Tessa sits up and stares into the distance. "I don't know. I don't know anything anymore."

thirty-nine

TESSA

It's still dark out as I gather Ethan's iPad and laptop, and slip out the garage door. I walk around the side of the house, feeling the cool night air on my face, lifting my hair from my forehead.

I walk down the wooden steps, and then I stand at the edge of the ocean. It's still choppy and swollen, as though someone pissed off Mother Nature—I wonder if she'd been cheated on, too.

The moon shines brightly, and I watch my skin turn silver with it. And then I heave the laptop and iPad into the ocean. I feel guilty for polluting. I never do. But in this moment, I have to get rid of these toxins. Ethan used them as vehicles of betrayal. He may not have meant to. He may really have stumbled down this rabbit hole and gotten carried away. I don't know. But I do know that I can't have these things near me, in my house. They have vile words on them, horrid pictures. I never want them to see the light of day again.

So now they're in the angry ocean.

I take a few steps back and sink to the bottom step. It's wet, but I don't care. I pull my knees to my chest and stare absently at the sea.

"Duke was adopted from a shelter," Lindsey says from behind me. "I'm sure they'll give you the names of the people who got him."

"How could you have done that?" I ask without looking at her.

"I don't know," she admits. "I guess it's why I said that maybe Ethan got carried away and acted out of character. I did, too. Normally I would never do something like that. I felt guilty, but I did it anyway. The whole thing . . . it made me a monster. And I'm thinking maybe it was the same for Ethan."

I ponder that. Maybe doing one terrible thing opens the door to other terrible things. Maybe it doesn't even start out as a terrible thing. Maybe it's a small thing, something almost nondescript, something just barely over the line. Then once a person does it and the world doesn't end, they take the next step.

Then the next.

Then the next.

Until they end up in the place where I am now, a twisted version of reality, far from where they started.

"Maybe," I finally answer. "The man I married wasn't capable of any of this."

"He's not that man anymore," she replies. "And you aren't that woman. The years have changed you. Children, businesses."

I fall silent. She might be right, my husband's young mistress.

"Anyway, we'll get your dog back," she says. "I'll make sure of it. I'll go to them and tell them I found his real owner. I'll get him back for you."

"That's the least you can do," I point out.

She's silent.

"Colt's going to be okay," she says a few minutes later. "I know you worry about him, but with his prophylactic treatments, he's in a good place. Those meds treat him before there's a problem. He's okay."

I blink slowly, trying not to say something mean. She's trying to be nice, trying to make things right. But she doesn't know what it's like to have a child with a life-threatening disease. She doesn't have the right to placate me, but deep down in my mother's heart, I know she's right.

I've allowed my worry for Colt to overtake me. To be the biggest thing in my life. It's possible that I did drive away my husband, at least a little bit. Not that I'm to blame for his affair.

I'm not.

He made that choice. At any given time, he could've come to me and expressed his feelings, but he didn't. That's on him.

"Ethan and I got married on the beach," I say aloud, remembering that perfect blue day in Maui. "It was beautiful. I thought that we had the world on a string."

"You *have* the world on a string," Lindsey replies.

"Maybe."

I'm exhausted. Mentally, physically, emotionally. I stand up and look at all the stairs leading back to my home. Slowly, I take the first step.

forty

LINDSEY

I stand at the kitchen door, watching the first fingers of dawn rise over the horizon. It's a new day. The irony is there; I'd be blind not to see it.

I'm numb. I'm in pain. I'm torn apart, yet things have never been clearer. I've inserted myself into a life where I don't belong, where I've never belonged. It's a mistake I won't make again.

Tessa moves to the sink, and the lights flicker. Then they go on. She smiles tiredly, and I see a bruise encircling her bicep. I think it's from my hand.

"Thank God. I'll make some coffee."

I don't care about coffee. I don't care about anything. I feel lower than I ever have. But Tessa makes coffee, and a few minutes later, she puts a cup in front of me.

"Drink," she tells me, just like she had with the whiskey. She slumps into the chair across from me, ragged, exhausted, and sipping from her cup.

281

I notice she has a tattoo on her wrist; it says *It goes on*. I wonder if she really believes that.

I point at it. "A tattoo? You don't seem like the type."

She chuckles wearily. "Maybe I'm not what I seem."

She thinks on that for a minute, staring at the black ink on her skin.

"I suppose they're truer than ever today," she decides. She reaches for her purse and then riffles through it. She pulls out a checkbook and starts writing. She tears the check out and hands it to me.

Pay to the order of: Lindsey Vale.

Amount: $20,000.

I look up at her, startled. "What the hell? What's this for?"

She puts the checkbook away and takes another sip of coffee.

"You saved my son's life. I would've pulled that wood out, and he would've died on the spot. I owe you. Walk away from here, Lindsey. Buy a plane ticket and go home. Get your son, and focus on him. That's how you're going to heal. That's how Logan will heal, too."

She gets to her feet and pauses, placing a hand on my shoulder, before she walks to Colt and sits with him again. I hold the check in my hands. I don't think I should accept it; I've taken enough from this woman.

Yet, at the same time, it was Ethan who took more. Tessa was right in the very beginning. He made the vow to her, not me. I regret the part I've played, though, and I tell her so now. I'm sorry for it.

She watches me somberly as I turn to her and cry.

"I know," she says simply, holding on to her boy. He's a man, yet a boy; broken, yet here and breathing. I watch the love she has for him, the way she holds his hand and covers him with the blanket, and I want that. I desperately want that.

He sought her out in a storm, in a moment when he couldn't even think straight, when he was dying. He came to find her.

I want to be that for Logan. I want to offer him a love that transcends oceans and time, a love that can withstand anything. He deserves that from me. I put the check in my pocket.

"Thank you," I say softly.

She nods.

I am not just talking about the money. But I think she knows.

forty-one

TESSA

The world is on its axis now, tilted and skewed.

I sit with Colt as he sleeps, listening as he breathes stronger and stronger. Lindsey sits in the kitchen, the girl I thought had tried to steal my life, who had . . . but hers was stolen, too.

Ava texts me. *Mom, are you okay? The storm was terrible.*

I answer. *Yes. I am!*

I'm not lying. I *am* okay. Or at least, I will be.

I bring Colt a bottle of water to drink, and he sits up, sipping at it with his eyes closed before he lies back down. I turn to Lindsey.

"Can you help me for a minute?"

She nods and follows me to my bedroom.

"I want to drag that outside." I point to the filthy mattress.

She doesn't even ask why; she knows. She helps me heft it up, and we shove it to the door.

The storm has died, and it is eerily quiet outside as we

use our body weight to pull the disgusting mattress out to the driveway.

"Can you do me another favor?" I ask, turning to her. She stares at me. "Can you go look in his closet and bring every shirt that he ever wore when he was with you?"

She walks wordlessly back inside, and I turn to stare at the ocean. Mere hours ago, it raged against the shore, and now, it is calm.

Just like me.

Lindsey returns with an armload of clothing. I try not to flinch at the volume that symbolizes how many days she was with him. Instead, I watch as she drops them on top of the mattress.

"He can't just walk away from this," she says.

I gaze wryly at her. "If you're suggesting we hold him hostage, the answer is no."

She starts to chuckle, but then she stops and stares at me.

"You do know that holding me here was illegal, right?" Lindsey's eyes are clear and bright, cutting into me.

I nod.

"You do know that sleeping with my husband was wrong, right?"

She nods.

"Shall we call it even?" I ask.

She thinks on that. Then quick as lightning, she draws back and slaps me across the mouth with all her strength. I see black spots and shake my head to clear them. My lip is on fire, and blood streams down my chin as she smiles at me.

"Now we're even."

My anger churns, but I *had* kept her handcuffed to my bed. On the other hand, she stole my dog and stalked my children.

I draw my hand back and slap her in the face. My palm throbs as it falls to my side, and her lips crack. The physical repercussion feels amazing in a primal sort of way.

"Okay. Now we're even," I agree.

We stare at each other for a minute before we each step back.

"Tessa," she says, turning to me, blood on her chin. "I work in an accounting office. I can tell you ways to . . . adjust Ethan's books. If you get divorced."

I stare at her, grasping her meaning—make him lose money, get him in trouble with the IRS.

"I think I've had enough illegal activity for a lifetime," I tell her.

She's quiet, then walks back into the house. She pauses next to Colt, watches him rest, and then disappears into the bedroom. She reemerges barefoot with her purse slung over her shoulder and her broken heels in her hand.

"Thank you for the money," she tells me at the door. She's so young, and in this moment, in the light of morning, she looks so soft, so vulnerable.

"You have your entire life ahead of you," I tell her softly. "You can do anything you want with it." She nods. "You can even hire someone to find your father. If you want."

Her head snaps up. Her nostrils flare, and her cheeks flush. She almost huffs as she breathes, then she relaxes.

"I'll think on it," she replies. "I've had enough cheating assholes for a lifetime."

I nod, smiling just slightly.

"Do you need help getting Colton out here for the ambulance?"

"No. I'm sure the EMTs will help. Thank you, though."

"I'm sorry," she says, her voice low.

There's a catch in my throat. At the beginning of this weekend, her sincere apology was all I'd wanted. Now I have it. Now we're done.

"Me, too."

She puts her hand on my shoulder, then gets into her car and drives away, in bare feet and my clothing.

I go back in the house and find my phone filled with texts from Ethan, begging me to give him a chance, to hear him out, telling me he's on his way. I have ten missed calls from him as well. I don't listen to the voicemails.

I don't know what I'm going to do. I glance at his texts.

You are my life.

I'll do anything to keep you.

I'll sleep in the garage, on the porch, on the beach, on the floor. I just want to be with you.

I've been so stupid.

Please, please, please forgive me.

Just give me a chance to talk to you.

I just touched down.

Please still be home when I get there.

On the one hand, I spent my entire adult life with that man. He's my best friend, the father of my children. He makes me laugh. He holds me when I cry. On the other, how could he have treated me like this? How can I ever forgive him and move on? How will I ever be able to trust him again?

I pivot, surveying my home. I don't see the gleaming hardwoods, the expensive finishings, the luxury. What I see is so much more than that. I see the lies created here, the hearts broken. My life was an illusion.

I'm on autopilot as I stare down at the pile of clothing and the mattress. Our bed had been the first expensive piece of furniture we'd ever bought, long before we could actually afford it. We'd spent so many passionate nights in this bed, so many lazy Sunday mornings. We had created children there; we had created a life.

And then Ethan had defiled it.

I run inside and grab a matchbook. I strike a match and toss it onto the bedding, onto the urine-soaked sheets, onto the shirts he'd been wearing when he'd been with Lindsey.

The flames rage orange and red, just like a sunrise. It's fitting.

Beyond the fire, I see the red flashing lights of the ambulance as it makes its way up the drive.

I look away, back at the fire, the flames that are burning away Ethan's sins.

My heart, surprisingly, is light. I suddenly realize that it's because I'm okay. One way or another, with Ethan or without him, I'm strong, and I'll be fine. I'll rebuild. I'll fix the wounds and shoulder the scars.

This will not defeat me.

It goes on.

I stare at my tattoo, at the truth in the words. And they *are* true. Life will go on. This will not break me.

The heat from the flames warms my face, and I smile.

acknowledgments

I would like to thank my dearest friends, the ones who held me up and kept me afloat when I faced my own nightmare. My two Michelles, Tiffany, and Gretchen. They listened to me, reined me in when I needed it, steered me in the right direction every step of the way. They kept me sane.

My friend, my hair stylist extraordinaire, my Julie. She knows what a strength she's been to me.

My husband should also be thanked. We weathered one hell of a storm, and learned so much about why people do what they do, and we lived to tell about it. Not only that, but we're stronger than ever. Without this happening, I would never have learned so much about myself, or realized how strong I really am.

I have learned that people are not simply black-and-white. We truly consist of a million shades of gray, some good, some bad, but all shades are human. As we examine those colors, our flaws, we have to remember that.

We can't control our feelings, but we can control what we do about them.

Stay strong.

Always.